"I accuse Alcatr... accuse Alcatraz of ... cuse Alcatraz of practices more fitting to the Spanish Inquisition than the United States of America! I accuse Alcatraz of something even more heinous than the murder of one man.

"I accuse the warden and associate warden and the institution known as Alcatraz of crimes against humanity. Willie Moore will not be the only defendant here. Alcatraz is on trial!"

MURDER
IN THE FIRST

DAN GORDON

BOXTREE

Published in Great Britain in 1995 by Boxtree Limited,
Broadwall House, 21 Broadwall, London SE1 9PL.

First published in the United States in 1995 by St. Martin's Press,
175 Fifth Avenue, New York, NY 10010.

Printed by Cox and Wyman, Reading, Berkshire.

ISBN 0 7522 0648 6

10 9 8 7 6 5 4 3 2 1

A CIP catalogue entry for this book is available from the British
Library.

For Jerry Zeitman—my friend, agent, partner and co-conspirator, who never gave up on this story.

ACKNOWLEDGMENTS

Though I like to think of myself as a supremely even-tempered and unflappable individual, I have been informed by those who know me best that the truth is otherwise. Being around me when I am working cannot be the easiest thing in the world. So the people who top any list of acknowledgments on this or any project with which I am associated have to be the ones who bear the brunt of living with it and me on a daily basis.

Jo-Ann, Zaki, Yoni and Adam are, as always, the rock and the reason for it all. They have my gratitude and all my love. My heartfelt thanks go to Lenore Marcus for the critical faculties, humor and forbearance of my frailties she brings to every project. Many thanks to David Thoreau, whose friendship I have treasured for 25 years and who toiled in the tombs and archives researching the original story in San Francisco.

This book marks the beginning of a relationship with St. Martin's Press and two gentlemen who have succeeded in making me feel awfully welcome. I cannot thank Roger Cooper enough for his graciousness and the speedy decision-making process he initiated with regard to this book. In a world of people who cannot make up their minds, he is an oasis of decisiveness. Likewise, I am grateful to Shawn Coyne, who has ridden herd on the publication of this book and whose collaboration on this and future projects are invaluable.

When I first got the idea for the motion picture of *Murder in the First,* Jerry Zeitman said "I know exactly who to take this to . . . David Wolper." David bought it in the room. For that and his guidance, taste and input, sometimes offered at ear-splitting decibel level, I will always be grateful, as I am for that of Bernie Sofronski and Mark Wolper, with whom I shared not only the adventures of the movie, but of a late-night landing in Tahoe to secure the opening that is finally being used in this book.

Likewise my appreciation goes to the entire Warners family, Terry Semel, Bob Daly and Bill Gerber, and to the folks at Canal Plus and Hexagon—chief amongst them, Marc Frydman. This story would not have seen the light of day were it not for Marc Rocco, who would not be dissuaded from directing the film version. I had the good fortune of being able to write this book after I saw the extraordinary performances of Kevin Bacon, Christian Slater and Gary Oldman, who brought dimensions to the characters that I never envisioned. My thanks also go to Grace Ressler of Warner Bros., Grace Reiner of the Writers Guild of America, West and Pierce O'Donnell and Robert Barnes for handling in an exemplary fashion the separation-of-rights issue, as well as to Lindajo Loftus who struggles to get the word out. Finally, to my first mentor Shlomo Karniel, who came to me one day and said "I have bad news . . . I think you're a writer."

MURDER
IN THE FIRST

Chapter One

IT DIDN'T TAKE LONG to plan it. Not even a minute. Not even thirty seconds. Maybe five, but probably less. The old man, the one they called the Wizard, had looked at one of those plastic trick eggs that you bought in the five-and-dime with the false cover that concealed half the egg in its top. He had set it down on the table, looked at the three youngsters, and said, "That's how you're gonna bust out of Alcatraz." Five seconds to come up with the idea. Eleven months, three weeks, four days, twelve hours, fifty-two minutes and thirty-seven seconds to plan it, to prepare it, to build all that needed to be built, always in secret and smuggle piece by tiny piece under the screws' noses.

There were three huge soup cauldrons in the main kitchen. When full, they bubbled over like witches' brews, steam rising, condensing on the windows, warming the kitchen on the coldest wet-cold Alcatraz day. The cauldrons were big enough to serve hundreds of bowls, but more important, each was big enough to hide a man—well, not a *man*. What man would hide in a soup cauldron? What man would fold himself up into the fetal position, burn palms and knees, and half suffocate himself in a soup cauldron? No, these were big enough to hide one *prisoner* each.

Then all they had to do after climbing inside was lower in the false cauldron, the "eggshell" they called it, after the five-and-dime trick. That was less than a foot deep and held only a few gallons but gave the illusion of regular garbage-can–sized cauldron full of broth.

They lit the fire for a diversion. The alarms went off and the confusion started as the guards evacuated one and all except for the three prisoners, Willie Moore, Avery Clark, and Willis Hanks, who hid beneath the false tops, the egg shells, the five and dime carney tricks and huddled there in soup pots as they heard the guards clear everyone and check the kitchen to make sure no one was hiding, waiting to escape.

They knew they would have only a few minutes at best to get out of the cauldrons and make their way to the incinerator chute inside the kitchen. There was no danger from the incinerator, it was lit only in the morning. They would inch their way down the chute, down into the burnt-garbage smell which was more intoxicating to them than any barroom hooker's perfume that promised powdered arms around you in the dark, for this one smelled like freedom.

At the bottom, the incinerator gate had been left

open by the guys from the day before, the guys who silently conspired for the payoff of knowing that some of their own were free, for the payoff of riding along with them in the dark, in their minds, in their cells, imagining themselves off the rock and back into the world where people had names.

When they hit the incinerator floor, Willie kicked the gate open and they felt the rush of black, wet fog as they crawled out. They ran, crouched low, beneath the sweeping light, jumped the low fence, and hit the drainpipe, shimmying down until they hit the beach. And then it hit them. They were outside the wall. They were free. No one on earth was freer than they were right now, at this moment, in this place, and no freedom anyone knew was sweeter.

They had won just as surely as any of the movie heroes Willie had seen at Saturday matinees and he wondered for a moment why there was no music, no triumphant swell of orchestra that was always there when the heroes won. But it didn't matter, because even if this was a silent movie, then still they were free until the searchlights popped on, exploding from patrol boats just offshore, lights scanning rock and sand from out of the darkness like space monsters on the radio shows, Willie thought. He liked listening to the radio shows a lot, but not as much as the baseball games. He would close his eyes when he was little and the world would go black and then he would light it from inside his mind and people it with ball-playing heroes or one-eyed monsters who shot out death rays, like the one that scanned down the line of rocks towards him now on this Thanksgiving night in Willie's twentieth year on earth, and third year as a prisoner in the federal penitentiary system.

Then there were the sirens. Avery Clark had not even waited for the sound. With the first glare of the searchlight, he raised his hands and shouted, "I give up! Don't shoot! I give up!"

Willis Hanks, for some reason that struck Willie as really funny, decided to run toward the water. It was almost like when Willie was a kid and at a creek behind the trailer park. He and his sister, Rosetta, would run to it and splash and dive from the rocks into the little pond until their father came, bottle in hand, cursing them both and their mother, too. That was how it looked to Willie, the way Hanks turned and ran toward the water, as if at any second he would look back to Willie and say just like Rosetta used to, "Come on in and swim, Willie, it's not that cold," and then they shot him. It was like a little red flower there suddenly on the side of his head, except that the other side where the bullet came out looked like hamburger, as he seemed to go up on one foot, arms outstretched, like a hawk set to soar high above all the troubles down below till he dropped beneath the waves and washed up on the shore like garbage.

Willie had never seen a man shot to death before. He had seen violence, he had felt it, he had waited for it and feared it, but he had never seen life end so quickly with such awful finality. A man ran into the water and turned into a corpse. So Willie panicked.

He took off running down the beach, arms pumping, blood rushing, wheezing foggy air in and out of his lungs, head ducked down, grabbing sand with toes, trying to outrun the death ray that swept along behind him in the black wet coldness that he prayed now with all his heart would swallow him whole and save him from the bullets.

Then he saw armed prison guards running toward him. He turned around and saw more coming from the opposite direction.

He had been free for less than thirty seconds. He stopped and put his hands up high in the air to show them they had won and that the game was over.

"Okay," he said. "Okay, it's over . . . I don't got a weapon!"

The guards drew closer to him. Among them he recognized Mr. Glenn, the associate warden. Mr. Glenn was smiling. So Willie smiled back. Mr. Glenn had won and Willie was not going to be a bad sport. He just wanted to know. . . .

"There was a snitch, wasn't there? That's how come you were waitin' for us. There was a sni—"

Before he could complete the word, Glenn hit him across the head with a blackjack. Willie sank down to his knees, hands covering his head, bleeding. Glenn hit him again and Willie said, "Okay, I'm down, I'm down!" It was like baseball: he was tagged, he was out. So why was Mr. Glenn still hitting him? And why was he still smiling? Then Willie's prayers were answered and blackness swallowed him whole.

Chapter Two

HE WOKE UP being dragged by two guards down the stairs leading to the dungeons. Mr. Glenn walked in front of them. The dungeons were cells which were little more than caves, carved into the rock of the island. Caves with metal doors. Metal doors with only a peephole and no window. Metal doors with a slat that could be unbolted and opened at the bottom of the door to allow food to be passed into the cell. The guards held Willie up against the wall as Mr. Glenn opened the door to one of the cells. Then Mr. Glenn turned to the guards.

"Strip him," he said.

With Willie standing half-unconscious against the wall, they pulled off his trousers and pulled off his shirt, and he shivered in his underwear, trying to fall back asleep and dream of blackness instead of waking to Mr. Glenn, who said, "Back off."

The guards left Willie against the wall and moved away. Mr. Glenn picked up a rusted metal bucket full of swill. Willie was starting to slide slowly down the

wall in sweet surrender when Glenn threw the bucket
and its contents, emptied it all, onto Willie who came
to with a start. Shivers now rattled through him like
skeleton teeth chattering.

Willie looked up at Mr. Glenn, who motioned for
the two guards to grab him. They took him under the
arms and dragged him toward the cell. He didn't resist, just turned and looked back to Mr. Glenn. He
had lost and he knew it. He just wanted to know the
final score.

"How long am I gonna have to do, Mr. Glenn?
How long? Huh?"

The inside of the cell was painted black. Black as
the darkest night, with no light but the pinpoint of
light coming through the peephole till it was filled
with the eye of Mr. Glenn. Then he moved away and
the peephole shut and all was blackness.

He sat there in the dark like a frightened lonely child
stuck into a closet by a father who had beat him.
Willie knew darkness. Willie knew closets. Willie
knew beatings and knew how to survive. He knew
enough to cry in silence. When they heard you cry, it
made them mad and they came back to hit you again.
It was that way with his father. It was that way with
the guards. It was that way with Mr. Glenn. Cry in
silence, don't make noise, don't let him hear it or
he'll be back. Gasp quietly, make no noise gulping
air. Be so quiet he forgets you are down here and
goes off to do something else, whatever it is that
grown-ups do when they're finished beating children.

Then survive it. Survive the darkness or it will kill
you, make you crazy. Use your ears. Use the sounds.

Use the smells and dampness on your skin. Make
them tell you what time it is. Divide the day from
night and you control it.

And so he listened for the guards, learned to tell
them apart by the sound of footsteps and the smell of
Barbasol on one and whiskey on the other. And every
time there was a new smell on the guard, or a new
sound encoded in shoe leather squeaks and nervous
feet tapping out their signature, every time there was
a new one of these it meant a shift had ended. Eight
hours had gone by. One third of a day could be
scratched off.

Two guards came down the corridor. One pushed a
barrel on wheels. The other carried a blanket, a flashlight, and a tear gas gun. They crossed over to Willie's cell and the guard with the flashlight pulled back
the bolt, opened the door, and scanned the cell with
his flashlight. The walls of the dungeon seeped seawater. Mold was growing. And then the light hit Willie. He sat huddled in the corner in his underwear,
knees knocking, teeth chattering, body shaking in a
million uncontrollable convulsions. He had nine days'
growth of beard. He hid his eyes from the light like a
primitive dodging the wrath of an angry God.

"Don't move or you'll get the tear gas. Got it?" the
first guard said.

Willie nodded his head and said, "Yeah."

The guard threw his blanket over to Willie. Willie
grabbed it, trying to stop shaking enough to pull it
around him.

"Thank you . . . Thank you," Willie said, as the
second guard came in and took the toilet bucket and

emptied it into the barrel in the corridor. "How . . . how long have I been in here?" he asked. He could do the time if they'd just let him know, how long. "I figure it's eight or nine days, huh? Is that it? How much longer I gotta do? Huh?"

The second guard threw the latrine bucket back into the cell.

"What's it gonna do—kill ya to answer me?"

The door slammed shut into blackness once again.

Mr. Glenn came down the stairs with the guard who shuffled. That's how Willie thought of him. The Shuffler. He could hear the shoe leather shuffle against the stone steps. Mr. Glenn and the Shuffler could hear Willie singing a piece of childhood doggerel. It was the kind of song children sang in the schoolyard, daring to be naughty.

" 'Oh, the monkey wrapped his tail around the flagpole . . . He caught a head cold right up his asshole . . . Oh the monkey wrapped his tail around the flagpole, he caught a head cold right up his asshole.' "

"He's been singing it over and over again," complained the Shuffler. "I can't get him to shut up, Mr. Glenn. It gets on your nerves, ya know?"

Mr. Glenn came barreling indignantly down the stairs and crossed into the corridor in front of Willie's cell.

" 'Oh, the monkey wrapped his tail around the flagpole, he caught a head cold right up his asshole.' "

"Shut up in there!" Mr. Glenn shouted. "You're breaking the silence rule! You're breaking a rule!"

And from within, " 'Oh, the monkey wrapped his tail around the . . .' "

Mr. Glenn pulled the bolt and opened the door and the dim light from the corridor was to Willie like a flood that blinded him with its brilliance so that he did not see the blackjack.

"You gonna shut up now?" Mr. Glenn asked and hit him. "You gonna shut up now?" Mr. Glenn asked and hit him. "Huh? You gonna shut up now!" Mr. Glenn asked and hit him. Mr. Glenn hit him many times, different times, times he wished he could predict, times he wished he could use to measure time with the beatings that were random, sudden and casual as a man might kick at a dog he kept around for kicking.

Willie, hey Willie boy, come on, Willie boy, Willie can you hear me? Come on pal, you and me . . . That's what the voice said. It called to him, came to him in the darkness when the kicking was done and it said, *It's not enough to figure out who's outside anymore and learn them by their shoe squeaks or the way they cough up phlegm and spit. You're not going to live through this if you stay down here. If you stay down here, you're going to die.* And then he would answer the voice, Where am I supposed to go? I'm in prison, in case you forgot. *Bust out,* came the answer. I tried to bust out, he told the voice. I've tried, Mr. Smartypants, and that's what got me stuck down here, if you hadn't noticed. Where am I gonna go and how am I gonna get there, if you're so smart? If you're so smart, answer me that one, huh? Where am I gonna go? And the voice said, *Inside, Willie, so far inside, so deep inside they'll never find you again. So far inside you can turn the volume up on the radio and listen to the ball game and they'll never hear it.* And so he did.

Willie Moore left his body and sank down into his soul and turned the baseball game up real loud till only he could hear it. He played them all, every game he'd ever heard. When the games were over, he ran the movies in his mind, saw the girls and heard them singing, saw the pretty things again and again, where no one else could see them, where no one else could hurt him. And when he ran out of baseball games, radio shows, movies, girls, and trading cards, he had numbers and all the tricks they could do.

Willie's head bobbed back and forth, back and forth, like a holy roller, as he said with more fervor than any pentacostal, "Eleven times eleven is one twenty-one, twelve times twelve is one forty-four, thirteen times thirteen is one sixty-nine, fourteen times . . ."

The door to the cell was opened. Standing in the doorway was a new guard next to the Shuffler.

"Get him up," the Shuffler said.

Willie huddled in the corner. They didn't see him well yet. Then the Shuffler pulled Willie to his feet and the new guard saw him. Willie's hair was down to his shoulders. His beard was full and his body lean as Jesus on the Cross. Willie closed his eyes against the light as they took him into the corridor. The light was blinding and Willie was dizzy and weak-kneed as a newborn colt or a dying one.

"Where . . . ?" he said. "What . . . ?"

"You get to go out," the Shuffler said.

"I'm through with it?" asked Willie. "I'm through?"

And he thought to himself he had won again. And again there should be music. He remembered to put in the music.

"It's a Christmas present," said the Shuffler.

They took him under each arm and started walking him up the stairs.

"Christmas," croaked Willie. "That's a lie. I . . . I been here longer than Christmas. I been here longer than Christmas. You can't trick me like that!"

Willie was starting to lose control. It was the kind of thing that he knew could get him beaten but he didn't care. He'd been in there longer than Christmas and they couldn't fool him. The new guard who was a little nicer guy, spoke softly to Willie, trying to calm him down.

"Willie," he said. "Willie, it's 1938 . . . Christmas, 1938. It's not a trick. You been down here a year."

Willie blinked at him, unbelieving at first.

"A year?"

"That's right," said the new guard.

"A year . . ." Willie said, and smiled weakly.

This guard was a nice man.

"You had me scared there for a second. I thought I was losin' it. I did it, huh? I did a year in the fuckin' hole an' I ain't too crazy, am I?" he said and smiled. "I did it an' it's done an' it's over."

Then the Shuffler spoke. "Moore," he said, "nothin's over. Thirty minutes—exercise—that's all you get."

Willie pulled back, hit with the injustice of it as hard as a blackjack. "Thirty minutes in a fuckin' year! He can't do that! He ain't a fuckin' human . . ."

"Hey, watch your fuckin' filthy mouth," the Shuffler said. "You don't want it, we take you back, asshole."

And if Willie's hands had been free he would have grabbed at the hand of the Shuffler to bring it to his lips, put his cheek against it, and kiss it. "No, no," he said, "I want it. I'll be good. I want it. I want it. Hey, that's the first time in a year I walked more than six paces without hitting a wall."

They led him up the stairs and Willie said, "They still got sunshine an' shit like that?"

Somebody broke my radio, he heard his own voice saying. Somebody broke my radio. Somebody broke my radio.

Don't talk that loud, said the voice coming back to him, in the hole. *Have you forgot everything I taught you? You make a sound and they'll know you're here and they'll come back. Mr. Glenn will come back. You don't want that, do you?*

No.

Then don't make a sound.

But somebody broke my radio.

What's that supposed to mean? the voice asked.

I can't get any baseball games on my radio. I can't get any funny shows anymore. I don't see any movies either. Nor any pretty things.

Well you know what's gonna happen if you can't hear your shows or see your movies, don't you? You're gonna go crazy and die.

Then what do I do? Can you fix my radio? Can you fix it so I'll see the movies once again?

No.

Then what *can* you do?
I can show you who to hate.
What do I do with that?
Make plans.
What kind of plans?
Plans on how to kill him, stupid.
Why would I want to do that?
Because, stupid, it's either him or you.
And the next time they took him up the stairs, he knew that it was Christmas yet again.

Warden Humson was a benign-looking man in his early sixties. He looked more like a college professor at a backwater university than the warden of Alcatraz. Humson's features were delicate, and behind his wire-rimmed glasses there was a warmth to his expression, almost kindness. He looked in fact, if one had to draw a comparison to a public figure, more like Woodrow Wilson than anyone else. He was a competent engineer.

There was a knock at his office door.

"Yes," he said, and turned to adjust an ornament on the small Christmas tree that stood near his desk.

Mr. Glenn came in. Mr. Glenn resembled Warden Humson in his dress and in the way he parted his hair. But there was no kindness in his face. And he looked, even to Humson, like a jailer.

"You wanted to see me, sir?" said Mr. Glenn.

"Yes, Mr. Glenn. Sit down, please."

"Thank you," said the jailer.

"Mr. Glenn," Humson said, "I've been going over the rotation figures in the solitary confinement cells."

Humson opened a leather-bound ledger that sat in

the left-most corner of his spotlessly neat desk. He turned the ledger towards Mr. Glenn.

"Is something wrong, sir?" asked Glenn, with no expression.

"Well, I don't know," Humson said, tapping his fountain pen on the ruler-edged line halfway down the page. "I don't think this can be right."

"What's that, sir?" Mr. Glenn asked in the tone of a smarmy butler who's missed a spot on the silver service and awaits his rebuke.

"Well, this on five-thirty-two," said Humson. "According to this, he's been there since November of 'thirty-seven. That's over three years."

Mr. Glenn tucked his chin towards his chest and then out again. "I don't believe there's been an attitude change with regard to five-thirty-two, sir. I haven't been able to see any."

"I think the man should be put back into the population," said the warden. "I mean, three years . . ."

Mr. Glenn squared his shoulders. His judgment was being questioned and he would stand behind his judgment the way others stood on principle.

"Five-thirty-two was the one who masterminded the escape attempt in 'thirty-seven. And there hasn't been an escape attempt since. I wonder if your rotation records show that? You let those animals think escape is possible and you might as well stick in a revolving door. Is that what you want . . . sir?"

As he spoke, Mr. Glenn betrayed the same steel in his look which made seasoned murderers cower in their corners. It was not without its effect on Humson, but he stood his ground as well.

"No, of course not," Humson said, averting his

eyes. "But three years . . . I think he's learned his lesson."

They brought Willie from his cell into the corridor. He looked insane. Said nothing. His hair and beard were long and matted with filth and mold. His eyes darted like an animal's as he squinted into the light. He took a step and stumbled and had to be supported.

They took him to the shower and he let the warmth hit him in the back of his neck, seep into his spine. They took him to the barber and cut his hair to prison length and the noise of the shaver buzzed like a hornet stuck inside his ear, boring into his brain, driving him crazy. They took him to the dining room and the sound of dishes banging, silverware rattling, was jarring to Willie, who jerked his head with each new sound.

It was the noise that hadn't been there before, because everything else had been. He had done this one hundred thousand times, maybe two hundred thousand. He had done it all. He had gone to the shower, he had felt the water, he had put on the new clothes and he had gone down into the population. Again and again and again, there in the hole down in his mind, he had walked up to a prisoner and said, Who was the snitch? The prisoner never had a face but always said something like, Willie, is that you? Welcome back, Willie. And he always asked it again, Who was the snitch? The prisoner understood. Nothing else needed to be said. Just who was the snitch and then the prisoner gave him the name.

A convict named Metz stood next to him in the food line, looked at him and recognized him.

"Moore?" he said. "Willie . . ." he said when he got no response. "We thought you was dead."

Willie still said nothing.

Then, as an offering, as a present, as the only piece of information Metz knew that Willie wanted, he leaned in toward Willie's ear and whispered, "There was a snitch. It was Clark."

Willie picked up his food tray and spoon. That's what they gave you in Alcatraz. Knives and forks were weapons. Willie said nothing as he walked over behind Clark, and Metz watched. Willie took his spoon, with the bowl part in his hand.

The handle stuck out like a knife. Then Willie dropped his tray. Everyone, including Clark, looked around at the noise. But for Clark, the look was too late. Willie lifted Clark's chin with one hand and plunged the spoon handle into the snitch's throat with the other. Then he ripped across Clark's throat, cutting through arteries, vertebrae, and windpipe so that the blood bubbled over and gurgled in Clark's trachea and his head was left there, hanging by what the guards said later looked like gristle.

Chapter Three

*T*HE UNITED STATES of America vs. *William Moore.* The judge, Henry T. Clawson, was a crotchety old fellow who viewed the courtroom as his private fiefdom. At one table sat Bill McNeil, the prosecutor. McNeil was a 35-year-old up-and-comer with tortoise-shell glasses, thinning blond hair, and the smile of a fat reptile who's just swallowed something smaller, whole. At the center of the room, Willie stood next to Bertram Russell, a befuddled-looking public defender with smudged spectacles, missing coat buttons, and the perpetual air of a man who's missed the last bus of the night. He was, in fact, the kind of defense attorney who made McNeil lick his crocodile chops in anticipation of fresh meat.

To all of this and the rich dark woods of the federal courtroom in which he stood, Willie Moore was oblivious. He stood rocking back and forth, back and forth, back and forth. The courtroom was empty of spectators, eliciting as it did very little attention amongst the members of the press or the habitués of the local legal goings-on. It was, after all, only the murder of a convict by a fellow inmate.

Judge Clawson held the indictment papers and there was heard in the courtroom the occasional snatches of his mumblings.

"William Moore . . . Avery Charles Clark . . . and there striking and wounding . . . sharp steel instrument . . . to wit, a spoon . . . A spoon?" he said looking up. "This can't be right. Is that right?" Clawson glanced over at Willie who said nothing, only stared. Then the judge looked back down at the indictment.

"To wit," he continued, "A spoon, about four inches in length, which, striking and wounding, described as aforesaid, caused the said Avery Charles Clark, thereafter, to wit, on December fifteen, 1940, to die."

Inside the San Francisco Public Defender's Office there was a cubbyhole which made most cloakrooms look as spacious as Windsor Castle. The desk was piled high with documents and a filing cabinet cut off any chance for pacing more than two steps in any direction other than the doorway, and then only if the door was open. The tenant, if not lord and master, of this Dickensian domain was Henry Willard Davidson, a baby-faced twenty-four-year-old lawyer with slicked-back hair and a prep-school manner that bespoke a privileged upbringing. His door was open and through it now walked Mary McCasslin. She was twenty-nine and a pretty woman. There was something country pure about her and her manner betrayed not ivy halls in East Coast schools, but open

fields of the San Joaquin Valley, or stretches of desert
outside of Tucson. Her hair was lacquered in the lat-
est style, and beneath the all-business look on her
face she could have been a movie star.

"Good morning, Mr. Davidson," she said
brusquely with a managerial air.

"Good morning, counselor," Henry said, with fitting deference to a superior. Then his eyes flicked
around the corridor and when he saw that no one
was looking, he closed the door with his foot and
pulled her around behind it, kissing her passionately.
Mary, with tact but firmness, pushed him back and
spoke in the whispers of a lady who wanted to keep
her job at a time when women lawyers were scarce
enough as it was.

"Henry, please," she said. "What if somebody
saw?"

"Then they'd know I was in love with you," he said,
trying to loosen her top-most button and simultane-
ously trying to edge his fingertips beneath the waist-
band of her skirt.

Mary expertly edged away, prying loose both sets
of searching fingers. "And I'd lose my job for fraternizing with a subordinate," she said.

"Oh, right. I forgot. You're the boss."

"No," Mary said. "You forgot I'm the only woman
who's ever been hired in this office and Henkin
wouldn't think twice about firing me." She straightened Henry's tie and smoothed back his hair.

Then it came to Henry in that one move, with that
smell of perfume on her wrist as she pushed his hair
out of his eyes. For just a moment, there was that
flash of his mother's hand, of the smell of her per-

fume upon her wrist, of her fingers moving a lock of hair out of his eyes and then it was gone. Those were the images he had of her. Fleeting, a noise caught, an expression captured, the hint of perfume lingering in the air. These were the things he could remember of her. Never when he tried, always when he wasn't looking. And the effect was always the same, he found himself looking like a little boy through the crowd for his mother's hand.

"Henry," Mary said, "are you listening to me?"

And it was over, the tiny movie ended in his mind, the shadow bleached off of the wall by the flooding light. Then he realized something was up. "What's going on?" asked Henry.

"I want you to look nice when you thank Henkin."

"The man's a cretin. Why would I thank him?" said Henry.

"He's given you a case."

"A case of what?"

Then the light bulb went on.

Mary looked at him, always surprised at how young he looked, much younger than the five years that separated them, and behind the youthful cockiness always was the fear. And then he got it. She could see it sweep across his face like the look on a child who says, A puppy? I get to have a puppy?

"A *case?*" Henry exclaimed. "I got a case? Henkin gave me my own case?"

"A Federal Murder One, no less," Mary said, adjusting the Windsor knot in Henry's tie.

But Henry could barely contain himself. "Mary!" he said, "I've been waiting all my life for this. I've been rehearsing my opening statement about an innocent man unjustly accused since I was seven years old."

Mary smoothed his suit jacket and tried to calm him down at the same time, "Henry, he's not unjustly accused."

"Sure he is," said Henry, indignantly.

Now Mary knew he was off and running and it was up to her to rein him in. Reality never seemed to cloud Henry's thought processes.

"He's a convict who killed another convict in front of three hundred witnesses."

"It was probably self-defense," Henry said.

"With a spoon," Mary said, definitively.

That snapped Henry out of it. "What with a spoon?"

"That was the murder weapon," Mary continued. "Your client killed the man with a spoon."

"What happened, did somebody make fun of his soufflé? Jesus!"

He was sulking a little now, and he didn't care who knew it. A guy waits his whole life to defend an innocent man and he winds up with the mad tablespoon killer.

"You do this one for experience, my darling," Mary said soothingly, "for the next time, when maybe your guy didn't do it. It's better to cut your teeth on a loser, you know. That way if you do make mistakes they didn't change anything. Now go see your client and make nice to Mr. Henkin on the way out."

Henry sighed. Mary had an annoying way of being right about most things.

"I'll pick you up at seven for dinner with my brother," he said, and walked straight into Henkin, the fifty-three-year-old lifelong bureaucrat who ran the public defender's office like a Stalinist commissar anticipating a purge.

"Good morning, Mr. Henkin," stuttered Henry. "I, uh, want to thank you, sir, for your confidence in me."

"I don't have any confidence in you," Henkin said, sucking a tooth. "The guy's guilty. A monkey could try this case and not make it any worse than it is."

"Yes, sir."

"Remember that," said Henkin, stabbing Henry's chest with a nicotine-stained forefinger.

"Thank you, sir," Henry said, wincing.

"A monkey!" Henkin shouted after him as Henry made for the stairs.

As he walked down to the city jail, Henry found himself working on his memoirs, composing them as he walked, the great look back at the illustrious legal career, the place where the book got really interesting, the chapter called, "My First Case of Murder."

Little did I know, he dictated in his mind, *as I walked down that familiar street that the meeting I was about to have would change not only my life, but more importantly, that of an innocent man unjustly accused of murder. As far as I was concerned on that cold December morning, this was just another day at the office. . . .*

The jailer received Henry at the elevator and walked him down the pea-green, chipped and fading corridor to the first set of barred doors.

There he was buzzed through, signed in, identified, and escorted yet further into the inner circle of the

century-old jail building. In the center of the great
room, stacked with tiers encircling barred cubicles,
there was a cage. It differed from the others in that it
was entirely made of metal. Not just the bars, but the
ceiling, too, was not really a ceiling, just more bars
welded onto bars, which in turn were welded into a
steel floor. Legend had it that it had once housed
Geronimo.

Henry tried to imagine the killer's face before he
saw him. It was both a conscious and unconscious
habit, this attempt to prepare himself for anything by
seeing it first inside his mind. He imagined Cagney
and Humphrey Bogart, Paul Muni or George Raft, or
maybe a pushed-in pug with a permanent smirk, a
nice little notch where you could fit a cigar, like Ed-
ward G. Robinson. Yeah, he was a tough guy, that's
right, a tough guy. He could imagine the nasal sneer,
the arch of the brow and the fighting cock stance. A
tough guy.

The cage there in the middle of the floor was built
to hold a tiger instead of the poor boy who sat huddled, clutching knees to chest, head almost imperceptibly bobbing, frightened at every sound, at any hint
of movement around him. Willie sat there shackled
hand and foot inside the cage with the look of one
who is insane.

"He's all yours," said the jailer to Henry, who fumbled in his briefcase for the file, trying to impress a
semi-comatose Willie Moore with his professional-
ism.

Henry cleared his throat. No reaction.

"Hi," said Henry.

No reaction.

"So, then . . ." Henry said looking down into the file yet again, as if he had a hundred such files of cases waiting to be tried in his briefcase. "Mister . . . Moore, is it?"

Willie said nothing.

"You are Mr. Moore?" Henry asked. "Is that correct?"

Nothing.

"Mr. Moore? That is your name, isn't it?" said Henry, taking off his glasses, looking at them as if he'd never seen them before and then sliding them back over the bridge of his nose. "William Moore?"

More nothing.

"Why don't I just assume it's your name until you tell me differently, how's that?"

It seemed like a fair enough deal, but still nothing.

"Uhh, Mr. Moore," continued Henry, "I will be acting as your defense attorney. My name is Henry Davidson and anything you tell me will of course be protected under the rules of confidentiality and privileged information of the attorney-client relationship."

Henry rattled off the pro forma as if that's exactly what it was instead of his virgin outing with his very own murderer. He pushed on. "So you can feel completely free to answer my questions in a totally honest and forthright fashion. Just for the record your name is Willie Moore, right?"

If sitting and rocking were a form of communication, one could call Willie Moore a talkative fellow. But as far as words went, he was giving none out for free.

"Stating your name is not an admission of guilt, Mr. Moore."

And then it hit Henry and he thumbed furiously through the file.

"Do you . . . do you speak English?"

His forefinger traced down the information sheet looking for place of birth. Where could this fellow come from, that he didn't understand plain English? From the looks of him, he might as well be a refugee from the dark side of the moon.

"It doesn't say anything in here about . . . I mean you speak English, right?"

Nyet, nada, zero, zip, nothing.

Henry put his face down so that Willie could read his lips, if that's what the problem was.

"Can you hear, I mean, are you deaf?"

Willie just stared straight ahead. His face was still half in the shadows.

"Uhh, look," said Henry. "Uhh, Mr. Moore, I'm your attorney, but I am not going to be able to provide you with much of a defense if one of us is catatonic, you see? We both have to, uhh, at least be able and willing to answer up when our name is called, you know?"

Then Willie looked up, not at Henry, just up, just enough to lift his head out of the shadows so that Henry saw the scar that ran down Willie's face, tracing the line of shattered eye socket and crushed cheekbone, of one eye blinded by repeated blows. And the other eye which only stared.

At the San Francisco Athletic Club later that day, Henry played a spirited game of squash against Bill

McNeil, the go-for-the-throat prosecutor whom he
would face in court. McNeil was a blue collar guy
who had worked awfully hard to hide his origins behind the right clothes and cars and things like squash
games, all of which came second nature to a rich kid
like Henry Davidson.

But behind McNeil's acquired mannerisms and
tastes, there still lay the reptile waiting for the kill.

"A continuance?" McNeil said, slamming the ball.
"Forget it, Henry."

Henry dove for the ball and came up empty.

"But he just sits there and stares," said Henry,
readying himself for McNeil's next serve.

"Maybe he's practicing for the gas chamber," said
McNeil. "Tell him to breathe deep."

McNeil let loose a killer serve.

Ace.

"You won't even consider a joint motion in the
interest of justice?" Henry asked.

McNeil planted himself for the kill. "Match point,"
he said. "No joint motion for continuance, no psychiatrist, and trust me, pal, no plea bargaining. Your
guy's gonna suck gas."

Wham! McNeil served. Henry dove. And the game
was over.

At 7:45 that evening, three-quarters of an hour after
he told his brother he would be there, Henry drove in
through the gate of his brother's mansion. There was
a circular drive and Henry parked the the 1939 Lincoln Continental Mark I out front. Then he and
Mary got out and crossed to the front door. Mary

looked up at the archway, the stonework, the gargoyles, and the leaded glass windows.

"I guess your brother does okay for himself," she said.

"It was our parents' house," Henry said, ringing the bell. "First-born inherits the big stuff. Very biblical, you know?"

Henry's brother, Byron, was a handsome man in his late forties who wore his success very comfortably. He sat in the imposing dining room beneath portraits of whiskered predecessors which lined the walls and lent the room the warmth of a trust company boardroom.

Henry looked around the room as if for ghosts, as if for some trace however fleeting of the mother or the father he knew had to have been there. He was sure there were memories in this room. He had heard of holidays of turkeys and Christmas hams, of servants bringing platters and of sherbert between the courses. His mother served sherbert between the courses, it was said, to freshen the palate. And he thought there should be some memory of that. What kid wouldn't remember ice cream served in the middle of a meal? But there was none, and the only image he had was a memory of something spilling, gravy, milk, or wine, spilling across the tablecloth and his brother's voice saying, "Henry did it."

"So, my dear," Byron said to Mary, pouring her a glass of a fine rich and very old Bordeaux. "I'm glad we've finally had the chance to meet."

"So am I," said Mary.

"I've heard so much about you," Byron said, pleased with Mary's look of surprise.

"Have you?" she said.

"Oh, yes, indeed. You're Henry's boss."

And he smiled at Henry, who stiffened in a most uncomfortable manner.

"Not really his boss," said Mary, reaching out instinctively to take Henry's hand. "I've just been there longer."

"Well," said the elder Davidson, leaning back expansively in the wing chair which sat at the head of the dining table. "I'm impressed. A woman lawyer in a senior position with the public defender's office. Very impressive. And I don't impress easily."

Mary looked him straight in the eye. "I'll bet you don't."

Byron returned her gaze and then turned to his younger brother.

He reached out a hand and, as if on cue, a liveried servant appeared with a teakwood humidor full of Cuban cigars. The servant opened the humidor and Byron without looking put his hand in and brushed his fingertips across a double corona, selected it, rolled it between his fingers, listening carefully for too little moisture or too much, took the cutter on the gold chain from his watch pocket, snipped the end, and handed it back to the servant like a tip. He rolled it back and forth, took another taste of the rich Bordeaux, and then again and without looking, found the matches without his fingers and set to lighting his cigar. It was the kind of ritual that one could imagine had been played out in this room by generations of robber barons who smoked fine Cubans while the ladies were excused.

"You see, Henry," he said, "I understand why she's

in the public defender's office. Woman attorney. Well, she doesn't exactly have a lot of choices. But you, you have a future!"

Now it was Henry's turn to take Mary's hand protectively. "Hey, Byron, why don't you just . . ."

But Byron moved even quicker and certainly more smoothly. "I'm sorry, my dear," he said to Mary, "I certainly didn't mean that the way it sounded, but I'm sure *you* see what I'm talking about."

He pointed to a muttonchop-whiskered gentleman in a portrait on the opposite wall.

"That old gentleman was our grandfather," said Byron. "He started our law firm."

"He was a robber baron," Henry said with disgust.

"He *ate* robber barons for breakfast," Byron said with obvious pride. "The firm he founded is now in its third generation. And I'm sure you're aware, Mary, that we are one of the most successful firms in this state. That's where Henry belongs. Henry and I are the only family each of us has. And the Davidson brothers—both of them—belong at Davidson and Winthrop."

He sipped at his wine and then turned from the woman to his brother.

"I mean you've got a Harvard degree, for God's sake. I ought to know, I paid for it and it's being wasted over there."

Henry had laid out the bait and for once Byron had taken it.

His brother's paw was in the trap, and Henry was looking forward to the snap of steel. "I guess that depends on your point of view," he said. "That degree right now, for instance, is defending a Federal Murder One. How do you like them apples?"

But instead of the anguished look of a newly trapped animal, Byron just smiled ever so slightly. "Considering why they gave you the case, I'd say those apples were on the green side."

"How do you know anything about—" Henry started to say, when his brother cut him off.

"Henkin called me," Byron said, and Henry was sure he could hear the clang of a steel trap springing on his own foot.

"What's Henkin doing callin' you about my case?"

"Sucking up to one of the most successful corporate lawyers in this state, that's what he was doing," Byron said, pausing to take another sip of the wine and then smacking his lips in appreciation of the vintage. "He'd kill to get a job at the firm."

"Yeah," said Henry, "Well, I believe in my client and I'm going to—"

"Your client," said Henry's older brother, "is a two-time loser who was sentenced for mail robbery to Leavenworth, tried to break out, was caught and transferred to Alcatraz as an incorrigible and there—"

Mary looked up in amazement. "How do you know all this?" she demanded.

Byron turned back to her and there was nothing snide there now, just the killer look of a bear protecting its one remaining cub. "My only brother is trying this case. I make it my business to know."

"You don't know anything, Byron," said Henry, realizing that his brother undoubtedly knew more than he did, but brazening it out nonetheless. It had always been this way. Byron had an almost magical way about him. Things came to him, not just easily, but as if by divine right. Henry could do whatever he wanted, plan whatever he planned, scheme whatever he schemed, it would all be to no avail. His big brother would forever be the big brother and Henry always just the kid.

"What did Henkin do, read you the highlights from the file?"

"No," Byron said smugly, "the D.A. did."

"Great," Henry said, getting up in disgust. "Just great." He threw down his napkin. This was more than just between brothers now. Henry could feel it welling up in him and he instinctively dug down to tap it, tap the energy and indignation, and more than anything else, the moral superiority which might finally let him kick his brother's ass. No, he told himself, this has nothing to do with my big brother and me. This has to do with the case, this has to do with justice.

"You want to hear about his great mail-robbery conviction? It was the height of the Depression. Here's a kid who was abandoned by his father, on his own since he's thirteen, just him and a ten-year-old sister and he's supporting her," Henry said, beginning to form the outlines of the defense in his mind. "He's in a drugstore looking for a job sweeping up. They don't have anything for him. The clerk steps away from the till. It's open. He reaches his hand around the side and grabs a five dollar bill."

As he spoke, Henry was there, could see himself in front of the jury, could see them sitting there behind a rail in front of him, could see how he would reach his hand around the other side of the rail like a magician grabbing rabbits from silken trick top hats. That's the way he would do it, his fingers plucking the imaginary fiver from behind the rail, and holding it up for the jury to see. Five bucks, ladies and gentlemen, five bucks. . . .

"Five lousy bucks," Henry heard himself say to his brother. "And it was just his luck that they had a rural post office in the drugstore, and *that's* what made it mail robbery! That's the big federal offense," Henry said not to his brother at all, but to the faceless faces sitting in the jury box in his mind.

"The point is—" said Byron.

But Henry wasn't paying attention any longer. He was busy making his plea. "They stuck him in Leavenworth, a seventeen-year-old kid, can you imagine what that must have been like? And when they tried to do what they tried to do, that is when he escaped. He never hurt anybody. Never touched a guard. And that's when they shipped him to Alcatraz. He's not exactly Al Capone, you know?"

"No," said Byron with the kind of look that ate robber barons for breakfast. "He's not Al Capone. All they had on Capone was income tax evasion. But they've got your boy on Murder One. It's a lost cause, Henry. A monkey could try it."

The next day at the city jail, Henry tried again with Willie Moore. Again, Willie sat there in the dark, head bobbing, hands clenched tight around his knees, drawing them into his chest, making no sounds, and from the looks of him, hearing none either.

"Look, Mr. Moore," said Henry, "I read your file and I'm trying to help you."

If Henry expected a response, he was disappointed. He could have as easily said, "I'm trying to hang you." Willie would evidently no more let himself be helped than hurt.

He sat there rocking, his one eye blind and the other unseeing, rocking himself if not to sleep then into a coma.

For his part, Henry pushed again, talking not so much to Willie as to himself. "I mean maybe there are extenuating circumstances in your case," Henry said. "Gettin' sentenced to Leavenworth for a five-dollar robbery, that's extenuating . . . Mr. Moore, I'm on your side okay? Do you understand that?"

Willie rocked back and forth in reply.

"Mr. Moore, you went and killed a guy so you're not catatonic. So I know you can talk or, or at least write, or if you can't write—somethin', just . . . somethin'."

I need some help here, pal, Henry thought. *This is for the memoirs, this is for the autobiography. You're the case and there's not gonna be any glory unless we both come out of this thing alive. So I need some HELP!*

Henry crossed over and looked between the bars into Willie's one good eye and said, "If you don't want to answer my questions we can start with something else. What do you want, Mr. Moore? There has to be something. It can't just be to sit there, because if that's all you do they're gonna stick you in the gas chamber. Don't you understand that?"

Willie's eyes flickered. There was no message, no

attempt at communication, but perhaps a hint of comprehension.

"You heard me," Henry said, "Didn't you? You understood?"

Willie's gaze focused a little better now.

"Come on, Mr. Moore," said Henry, "come on . . ." he said, as if cheering on a last-place horse that had finally begun to make its move.

Willie's mouth twitched and then the lips began to almost form a word, silently, but the nerve synapses seemed, at least to Henry, to be connecting.

"Haaooo," said Willie.

Henry just looked at him. " 'Haaooo.' What . . . what are you saying? 'Haaooo.' "

"Hhhhooww . . ."

"How?" Henry said. "How? Are you saying how?"

"How," said Willie.

"How . . . ?"

"How . . ." Willie said again.

"How," said Henry. "What are you, a fuckin' Indian? Come on, Mr. Moore, don't quit now. How, *what?"*

Willie turned not to Henry, but at least in his direction. He connected words like a child taking its first steps. "How . . . is . . ."

"How is who, Mr. Moore?" said Henry, holding his hands out to Willie. "You want to know how somebody is, I'll find out."

"How is . . . DiMaggio?" Willie said, and there at the corners of his mouth was a grimace or a smile.

"DiMaggio," Henry repeated. "How is DiMaggio? Who's DiMaggio? Is he a prisoner?"

Willie turned now completely to Henry, as if this

finally was important. This, above all else. "How is DiMaggio doing this year . . . ?"

Henry stepped back, puzzled. That couldn't be what he'd meant. Could it? Could this point-one IQ specimen possibly be talking about a game? Is that what could be occurring here? While he, Henry Davidson, defender of the downtrodden and the oppressed masses of the earth was trying to bring about an end to injustice and win a victory for all freedom-loving peoples everywhere, could this cretin possibly be talking about a *game?*

"DiMaggio?" Henry asked, betraying none of his silent indignation. "The—the—the baseball player?"

And when he said, "baseball player," it was with obvious disappointment if not disgust.

But Willie Moore was not tuning in to nuances. He nodded his head slowly, almost happily. He had heard the sound of the great hero's name repeated four times now, and the images slowly formed in his mind, the sound of the crack of the bat, the excited announcer's voice, and the fans cheering.

"How is Joe DiMaggio the baseball player doing this year?" Henry asked incredulously. "Is that what you're asking?"

Willie nodded his head again, unmistakably pleased.

"You mean what his team's doing and stuff like that?" asked Henry.

Willie nodded his head in an excited way. He was Dopey the dwarf inclining his bald head for the sweet caress of Snow White's kiss. He was every stupid dog wagging his tail for a bone.

"Yes," Willie said. "Yes." And he leaned in toward

Henry, expectantly, waiting for the news, a garrison surrounded, about to get word of reinforcements.

"Uhh," said Henry. "Uh, I, I don't really follow baseball, ya know?"

There was a moment and then the window closed, and Willie Moore leaned back, disgusted, back into his trance.

"Mr. Moore?" said Henry. "Mr. Moore . . . ?" But his client was gone.

Chapter Four

HENRY DAVIDSON SHOULD have been walking with a determined, professional air down the street. There should have been an intensity, a focus to his every step. But to the casual passerby he would have looked not like a knight on a charger riding off to crusade for his client's rights, rather he would have looked exactly like what he was: a baby-faced dreamer. For he was approaching the building that had been both refuge and temple to him as a child. It was the place where he went, ironically enough, both for safety and adventure. The safety lay in the rich leather and binding smells, in the warmth and comfort of a favorite table and chair tucked away in its own lovely alcove, to be piled high with books. And it was from the safety of that warm place through the medium of those very books that young Henry set forth with the great Hawkeye, last of the Mohicans, with Ivanhoe, Arthur and young Lancelot, with Robin Hood, Davy Crockett and Jim Bridger, with cowboys and knights, conquerors and sword-fighting

poets to defend truth, beauty, and honor; to defend
those who could not defend themselves and to win
for them and the downtrodden of the earth, liberty
and justice for all. And it was here, too, that he would
follow the exploits of a more corporal hero, the great
Darrow the greatest trial lawyer, the greatest pleader
for justice the nation had ever known. He would read
the speeches of Darrow, Zola, and Webster and
imagine that they were his own, imagine that it was
he who stood before the bar of justice and pled the
case that would change the course of history. As he
walked up the steps of the San Francisco Public Library, Henry Davidson was ten years old again and
ready to conquer the world.

All his life he had prepared for this, for the day
that he would walk into the great library, the once
skinny squire now magically transformed into stal-
wart knight. He had dreamt of the day when he
would walk to the shelves in the beautiful old, oak-
lined building to take out volumes of the law which
he would use to free an innocent man. But he did not
stop at the stacks of bound court cases. He crossed
instead to the bespectacled librarian and said, "I'd
like to see all the papers for 1938, 'thirty-nine, 'forty
and 'forty-one. The sports sections."

And when he said it, he sulked. Oh, the indignity
of it, to stand there looking like a lawyer and ask for
tinker toys. It was humiliating. It was a dunce cap on
his head and rotten lettuce thrown past the foot-
lights. It was the cutest girl at the cotillion saying,
Dance with *you?*

She returned with the papers and a smirk and he
wanted to tell her it was for a client in a federal

Murder One, a catatonic cretin who stood between
him and the most important case since Darrow defended a small town teacher's right to discourse on
Darwin instead of Deuteronomy, but instead all he
said was, "Thank you."

Then from the stacks to the wonderful old revolving door across the marble floor that echoed with
each footfall, he dictated into his memoirs, *It was
then I realized that this was for a client in a federal
Murder One, et cetera, et cetera.*

This time exiting the library, Henry walked not like
a ten-year-old, but like a lawyer whose memoirs were
on the best-seller list, who was on his way to see yet
another desperate client.

Later that day in the city jail, Willie sat as before, as
always, arms hugging knees, a fetus unwilling to be
born, head rocking to and fro upon his cot. Henry sat
opposite him with a stack of notes and newspapers.

"DiMaggio had a great year," Henry read from his
legal pad, sneaking a glance at Willie to see if there
was any reaction. When he saw none, he continued,
undaunted. "He was the American League batting
champ with a three-fifty-two average which was just a
little bit off last year when he had a three-eighty-one
average."

There was still no reaction from Willie. So Henry
bent over and picked up one of the newspapers and
started to read aloud.

"October nine, 1938. The thirty-fifth annual World
Series came to a predictable end today with the New
York Yankees beating the Chicago Cubs in a four-
game sweep that sent the Cubbies reeling, proving

once again what many have said all along: the Yankees own the series with this their third consecutive world championship. The American League champs were in charge from the first pitch of the series . . ."

Willie sat there, catatonic, but as Henry read, Willie slowly turned his head and leaned in a bit. Henry saw it, smiled to himself, and continued reading.

"Led by pitchers Red Ruffing, Lefty Gomez, and Monte Pearson, with the batting power of catcher Bill Dickey and second baseman Joe Gordon, both batting four hundred for the series with six hits apiece, and center fielder Joltin' Joe DiMaggio . . ."

Four hours later, the stack of papers at Henry's feet had been reduced to just a few editions. Henry had read the results of every game played in either league for the last three years. Willie imperceptibly, had left his fetal position and was bent forward, looking not at Henry, but listening intently.

"October eight, 1940. The Cincinnati Reds came back from being down two games to three to win their first World Series title in twenty-one years with a two-to-one win by Paul Derringer in Game Seven. But it was Bucky Walters in the sixth game who . . ."

"How old?" said Willie suddenly.

Henry looked up, unbelieving, but there it was, Willie looking straight at him.

"What?" Henry said. "Mr. Moore, did you say something? Willie?"

When Willie spoke again, it was haltingly. He looked Henry up and down, seeing him so it appeared, for the first time, almost surprised at his presence.

"How . . . old . . . are you?" Willie asked. His

voice was pure gravel, like he had gargled with carbolic acid.

"Me?" said Henry, "I'm—I'm twenty-four."

Willie looked at him for what seemed like a long time, looked at the baby face and the smooth skin, at the well-cut suit spun of wool, at the tie made of silk, at the starched white collar, at the little spectacles that had never been broken by a fist crashing into his face, at the razor-cut hair that hung so fashionably down into his eyes, in that boyish way that mothers and girlfriends brushed back with perfumed hands. Willie reached out and pulled Henry's hand toward him and saw the gold cufflink peeking just beyond the sleeve of the perfectly tailored coat, saw the graduation watch that said, Rolex Oyster on its face, saw the manicured hands free of scars or callouses or the broken bones that betrayed signs of torture.

Twenty-four, Willie thought to himself. And then he spoke. "I think I am, too," he said.

Judge Clawson glared down at Henry from behind the bench.

"Your Honor," said Henry, sounding far too much to his own liking like Oliver Twist with an extended empty bowl. "The defense respectfully requests a continuance of sixty days to—"

But before Clawson could reply, McNeil broke in, rising from behind his desk.

"Your Honor," said the prosecutor, "he doesn't need sixty days. The facts of this case are so simple that even—" His voice dripped with sarcasm and Henry felt compelled to cut him off before he could complete the thought that even a monkey could try this one.

"Your Honor," Henry said, "the man has been almost catatonic since I met him. Yesterday was the first time I even got him to—"

But if anything, McNeil was more competitive in the courtroom than on the squash court. He played now as much to the jury as to the judge. "He wasn't so catatonic he couldn't walk over and slit a guy's throat in front of two hundred witnesses."

"Mr. Davidson," said Judge Clawson, leaning forward and peering over the tops of his spectacles, "is it your contention that the defendant is insane? Is that what you mean by catatonic? Is this laying the groundwork for a not-guilty-by-reason-of-insanity plea?"

Henry moved out from around the defense table and approached the Judge's bench like a jester to a monarch. "I don't know yet, Your Honor," he said. "I've never even talked to him about the case. The closest I've got is—"

"One week, Counselor," the Judge broke in, "and then you are either to tell me you are ready to come to trial or you come in here with a request for a competency hearing."

"But, Your Honor . . ." Henry pleaded.

"One week!" Clawson all but bellowed, and McNeil smiled his crocodile-basking-in-the-sun-at-the-river's-edge smile.

In Willie's cell at the city jail, Henry read and slowly, bit by bit, engaged Willie in conversation. They talked, it seemed to Henry, of nothing. They talked of numbers and letters which held no meaning let alone glamour, let alone allure, let alone adventure, excitement, heroics or inspiration for Henry. RBIs and ERAs 240, 280, 360, and amazingly, 410. Who cared? And all the while, what Henry wanted was to speak of broad concepts, of learned men who used words in defense of ideas, who used ideas like swords in defense of ideals, for whom ideals were everything and baseball was nothing. He was in fact looking for the same bullshit sessions he missed so much from Harvard. Just as Willie must have missed, Henry thought, whatever it was that people like Willie missed. How could he possibly find the statistical averages, recorded instances of wood hitting hurled leather-covered cork-and-twine of interest. And yet, Willie smiled like a Buddha, as if each set of baseball statistics were the essence of enlightenment.

Finally, Henry decided it was time to talk about the case, about matters more important than a game, about life and death.

"Mr. Moore, you and me have got to talk now," said Henry, "you know?"

Willie looked over at Henry, and for once he was not retreating. He was there in the jail cell with his attorney. He had heard a question and Henry had every reason to expect that his client would respond.

"Mr. Moore," he said, "did you kill Avery Clark?"

Willie sat on the cot with Henry's newspapers in front of him. He fingered them absently, ignoring Henry.

"Joltin' Joe DiMaggio," Willie said in a kind of cadence. "Joltin' Joe DiMaggio."

Henry was not about to let him slip away. "Mr. Moore," he said sharply.

It worked. Instead of slipping back into the trance, Willie looked up and for once, there was even a kind of expression on his face, perhaps anger, perhaps disappointment, but emotion nonetheless.

"Don't call me Mr. Moore," Willie said.

But Henry was not going to take time out for niceties or salutations or proper forms of address.

"The single most important thing I need to know for your defense—" Henry said.

"Willie," Willie said softly. "Call me Willie."

And when he said that, it was a prayer.

In retrospect, it was in fact for Willie, the single most important thing in his life, to be called by a name and not a number, to be treated not just as a prisoner, but maybe for once, and just for awhile, as a friend.

But if you have not been a number instead of a man, if friendship is something you have taken for granted as easily as food and shelter, a warm bed, and the clear and certain knowledge that the morning will not find you grubbing through garbage for bits of food, then perhaps like Henry, you would be excused for not realizing the importance of being called by your name.

For to Henry, as to anyone else who had not lived the kind of life imposed on Willie, a name was just the way you started or punctuated a sentence and what was important was the line of thoughts in between those two points. The opposite was the case with Willie Moore. Thoughts were what you feared in

the dark and a friend was what you hoped for with all
your heart.

"Willie," Henry said, tossing the name off like an
overcoat to be shed in a warm room. "Fine. I'll call
you Willie. Now, Willie, your defense is going to
hinge on—"

"Hank," Willie said. "I'll call you Hank."

Again, Henry was oblivious to what was in effect
his christening. He was, after all, a lawyer, not a
friend.

"Did you kill Avery Clark?" he asked, and then
remembered to add, "Willie."

"I had a dog named Hank," Willie said with a
dreamy look.

"What?" Henry asked.

"Willie and Hank," Willie said, smiling, nodding
his head back and forth, rolling the sound of the
names around in his brain with evident pleasure.
"Willie and Hank," he said, luxuriating in the com-
panionship of it all. "Willie and Hank, just shootin'
the shit, huh?"

All right, Henry thought to himself, it's almost like
the Bedouin cultures he had read about in anthropol-
ogy class, certain social formalities must be followed
before one could get down to the business at hand.
So Henry reached into his briefcase, pulled out an
unopened pack of Luckys, undid the cellophane,
tapped out a cigarette and proffered it to Willie.
Cons love cigarettes, the thought flashed through his
brain. *It's part of their culture, and I, Henry Davidson,
have taken one step towards being a more experienced
criminal lawyer. Always offer the criminal his cigarette
first.*

"Would you like a cigarette, Willie?" Henry said. They were children really; it was almost like offering candy.

Then Willie looked up and there was the tiniest hint of a smile on his face. "No, thanks," he said. "That shit'll kill ya." Then he laughed at his own little joke. "That's kind of funny, that shit'll kill ya."

And inside his mind, Willie was giddy. He was dancing. He was delirious as a homely boy who just heard *yes* from the lips of the prettiest girl in class, as delirious and giddy with the joy of acceptance and belonging as any little brother whose big brother just let him tag along, as giddy as an orphan taking his newfound parents' hands, as giddy as a boy who'd spent three years in darkness and in silence and had just told a joke, finally, to a friend.

"Willie," Henry said, assuming that since the cigarette had been declined the formalities had now ended, "did you—"

But Willie cut him off. "Cause I'm gonna die anyway in that gas chamber," he said. "So that's a joke, huh? That shit'll kill ya, that's kind of funny," Willie said and watched him, oh so closely to see how this gift of joke had been accepted or declined, to see if the girl took the flowers or the brother took the ball and said, Yeah, I'll play catch, to see in fact if he had a friend or was still alone.

As for Henry, now he saw an opening, a way in which to begin their relationship, that of crusading lawyer and properly grateful, worshipping client. "Mr. Moore," Henry said, and then remembered. "Willie . . . I'm your lawyer. I'm going to defend you. If I have anything to say about it, you are not going to die in that gas chamber."

Willie looked at him as if he were crazy. "Sure I am," he said simply, stating what for him was a fact of life or, in this case, death. "Mr. Glenn told me so."

"Glenn?" asked Henry, "The associate warden? When? When did he come here?"

But Willie was not so much answering as continuing in his reverie. "He said it's brand-new. He said they're gonna try it out on me. He came all the way down here just to say that."

Willie shook his head at the thought of that and started to retreat into himself again, pulling his knees up and turning away. But Henry was not about to lose him.

"Oh, no you don't, Willie," he said. He wanted to reach out and take him by the arms, but the truth was, Henry was afraid of him, afraid of the kind of guy who could walk over and, without warning, rip your throat out with a spoon handle. So he didn't touch him. He just said, "Willie, look at me. I'm not going to let them put you in that gas chamber, but we've got to talk. You've got to help me, so I can help you. *Willie?* Did you kill Avery Clark? Willie? Talk to me. Did you kill Avery Clark?"

Willie turned slowly and looked over at Henry as if just waking up from a kind of sleep. An idea was forming slowly in Willie's brain, more than an idea, a question. A great deep mystery to which Willie could see no logical answer and to which he attached all measure of importance, as if the reality he had worked so desperately to construct for three years in darkness could be shattered now, dependent upon

the answer. This was more than just a matter of potential friendship. This was the stuff of which cata-
clysms were made, as if some underpinning of belief
held the world in balance on its axis, as if its denial
could launch the planet out of orbit, careen wildly to
the sun and kill them all.

"How?" he asked. "How could you not know
about baseball?"

"What?" said Henry, not able to make the leap
onto that particular train of thought.

"You said," Willie said, trying to remember the ex-
act words, " 'I don't follow baseball.' How could you
not follow baseball?"

Well, okay, thought Henry, he's crazy, and the way
you deal with crazy people is to hit them over the
head with sanity. "Willie," he said, determined to impose reality upon the poor maniac in order to save
him from himself. "Willie, did you kill Avery Clark?"

"Over and over," said Willie. "I don't know, musta
been a year, maybe more all I did was hear 'em in my
head . . ."

Willie was quiet, with a kind of reverence for the
voices that had spoken to him, as reverent toward his
voices as the martyred Joan was toward hers, for they
had come to him in the dark to comfort him, for they
had saved him.

"I don't know what you're talking about, Willie,"
said Henry. "Are you talking about Clark? What are
you talking about?"

Willie looked at him with a look that mirrored exactly that of Henry, a look that said, Are you out of
your mind? "I'm talking about baseball," he said, as
if that were self-evident. "I'm talking about the great

American pastime. All I did in there was go over every game I ever heard on the radio, playin' over and over in my head, and you had all those games to go to and you didn't even care?"

"Willie," said Henry, determined to bring him back from dreams of baseball into the reality of murder, "I'm talking about Avery Clark."

And here it was as if Willie's head exploded from the overabundance of images from the ongoing war between the forces of light and the forces of darkness, from reality self-imposed inside a hole to save his life, from visions of murder, torture, beatings and privation, to noble heroes hurling balls on diamonds bathed in summer's golden light.

"I'm talking about three fucking years they had me in solitary, man!" he bellowed. "Three fucking years without any fuckin' light even, and you had all them games to listen to and you don't even know what Joe DiMaggio hit this year? What kinda asshole are you?"

It was as if the realization had just now hit Willie. He had been in there for three years! They had kept him in a hole carved into a rock, sealed over with a door made of steel for three years. It wasn't about baseball, it was about Alcatraz! And as it hit Willie, so too, finally, the horror of it all, the sheer, unmitigated horror hit Henry as well. Three years in a pitch-black hole. Three years. Three years.

Chapter Five

HENRY AND MARY pulled up in a cab in front of a very impressive office building which was all the more impressive because of its name, the Davidson Building. Mary glanced discreetly at the nameplate riveted into the wall beside the revolving door. Henry saw it and secretly reveled in it. As much as he liked to deprecate the family fortune, he knew only too well that there were few things in life as impressive to a career woman as your own building. Cars were flashy, buildings were better.

"He's your only family, Henry," she said. "He cares about you."

"He's a royal prick," Henry replied, "But he's the best lawyer I know and it's gonna take somebody that good to tell me if we've got a chance for some kind of insanity or diminished-capacity plea."

This was the best. If he had planned this day for months, it could have been no better. If he had schemed and maneuvered, altered schedules and formed secret alliances, it could not have been im-

proved upon. He was still very much in the wooing
stages of his relationship with Mary, who was after all
the beautiful older woman whom he hoped to marry.
And if not, at least to have the kind of affair that
years from now, he would look back upon in smoky
bars with sloppily sentimental piano stylings and say,
That was the one.

So here he was with a career-minded liberal who
admired Eleanor Roosevelt and yet knew the value
of financial security. And who was he and what was
he doing? He was the rich kid selflessly working in
the Public Defender's office on the way into the
building which bore his name and implied the rock-
solid, blue-chip privileged status into which he had
been born as if in a state of grace, which all the while
he bad-mouthed as having come about because his
predecessors were corporate oppressors of the
masses. Yet he on the other hand was both so idealistic and pragmatic that he swallowed down his distaste
for his own wealth in order to seek the counsel of his
capitalist pig brother, but only in the pro bono service to his Steinbeckian damn near Joad family client. Though truth to tell, there was no doubt that of
the two of them, Henry looked an awful lot more like
Fonda than Willie, a fact he assumed was not lost on
Mary, either. And the best part of it all, he told himself, was that none of it was artifice and all of it was
true.

Thus Henry and Mary entered the Davidson Building which bore the name Mary saw emblazoned there
in bronze and hoped someday to make her own.

The offices were as impressive as the family mansion. An abundance of oak and brass guarded over by

a matronly looking lady in her late fifties, whose name was Irene, and who, one could assume, not only knew in which closet every skeleton was located, but who may well have been the person assigned by the family to put them there. She was the kind of rare and valued employee whose only family was right there in that office.

"Hiya," said Henry like a long-lost nephew to a favorite aunt.

Irene lit up when she saw him. She stood and held open her ample arms and hugged the prodigal son who had finally come back to the family manse.

For Henry, the images of his mother and father were fleeting shadows on the wall, ethereal pictures fading in his mind of elegant hands and perfume that came closer as the kiss good night approached, of the rich tobacco smell that clung always to his father's coat, of liquid spilling across holiday tables and reflections of himself in polished hub caps looking back at him from his father's chauffeured Lincoln.

The images of Irene, on the other hand, were solid, warm and fleshy. They were plentiful and always reassuring. Hers was the hand he held, hers the adoring look shining back in the audience of school plays when his parents were gone and his brother was busy, her apartment the fabled dream place of his childhood, the place of mystery and wonder that children all reserve for the places where they're loved without condition. He had spent weekends there and holidays there, he had run away and wound up there. She had let him use her meat grinder clamped onto the wooden table in the kitchen where he turned the cheapest steaks magically to ground round with onions ground into the meat and eggs and ketchup and all the bread crumbs that made the meat go further and became, as if by magic, the entire world's best meat loaf.

"You feel bony," she said, like only a mother or nanny could say. "Have you been eating?" Then she looked over at Mary. "Has he been eating?" she asked.

"Why do you ask her? How do you know if she knows?" said Henry in the offended tone of little boys whose mothers know their secrets. He was on his own now, he had his own apartment, he was no longer in school. He needed no notes from home, he had beer in the ice box and even if he was disinherited entirely in the next thirty seconds, he drew a salary and was a man of his own means. If he ate he knew it, if he didn't he was equally conversant with that fact. His eating and not eating had only to do with him, not with whether or not he was being fed, taken care of, looked after, supervised, mothered, mistressed, or wifed in any way. It seemed to Henry upon reflection that every bit of freedom he had won had been hard fought and taken over by him from some woman, whether she be teacher, nanny, den mother, dorm mother, or Irene. And now that he had his first taste of adult, grown-up, free-of-Irene-at-last freedom, here she was handing him over to Mary! Why *did* Irene ask her? How *did* she know if Mary knew?

"I don't," said Irene, giving Mary the once-over with a practiced eye, "but she looks like she cares and that's good enough for me."

Mary smiled and held out her hand, hoping for an

ally, hoping in fact for someone who would pull Henry aside and say, Don't let that one slip away, she's got a head on her shoulders and she'd make you the wife you need.

"You must be Irene," Mary said.

"And you must be special," Irene replied, "if he brought you here."

"She is," said Henry, putting his arm around Mary and not noticing Mary's discomfort at trying to choose between being a lawyer or the heir apparent's girlfriend. "Irene," Henry continued unaware of her plight, "this is Mary McCasslin. Irene is the real power behind my brother's throne. She's been with this firm longer than he has."

Irene smiled warmly at Mary and decided that the latter was, without any doubt, the girlfriend. "And I've known this young man since he was in diapers. And I changed quite a few of those diapers, too," she said and instantly changed Henry once again, this time from the idealistic lawyer/suitor and, in short, man into a boy.

"Is he in?" Henry asked in his lowest voice, nodding towards the closed oak door, in what he hoped was his most businesslike of tones.

"He's got meetings," said Irene. "But if you need him they're about to be canceled."

"I need him," Henry said in a firm voice, "So does my client."

Irene's smile could have lit up a dungeon as she turned to Mary and said, "He's been waiting to say that since he was seven years old."

"I know," said Mary, and the bond between them was made.

They had Henry in common and Henry hated it
and loved it both the same. Hated it for turning him
again before their eyes into a kid and loved it just like
any little boy turning cartwheels for his mother, who
was after all, when it was said and done, the fountain-
head of all loving approval.

Byron leaned back expansively in the overstuffed
brown leather chair that sat behind the massive an-
tique desk which had been brought out from Chicago
on the first train to cross the continent, by Byron and
Henry's grandfather. There were cigar burn marks
along the leather arm rests and stains of cognac and
wine, spilled in opulent reveries or midnight contem-
plations. There was a history to this chair that you
could touch and feel and smell, that spoke of white
man's power, of ambition and achievement, of conti-
nents conquered, and blood spilled in the name of
destiny recognized, embraced and then hard fought
for, realized and won, no matter what the cost or
profit. And now the chair was Byron's.

"Insanity," Byron said, looking at Henry and his
lawyer/girlfriend across that desk that coolies had
sweated under as they off-loaded it from one train to
the other. "Diminished capacity. They're not gonna
work."

"Why?" asked Henry.

"Because," said his brother, leaning back into the
leather that fit him like a glove, "the man was sane
enough to walk over and rip the guy's throat out
calmly and coolly." Byron paused to snip the end off
a cigar and then engage in the kind of foreplay which
was as much a part of the cigar ritual as the smoking

itself. It bespoke leisure and taste, connoisseurship and reward. It was the stuff of oak-lined rooms and men so powerful a nod in one direction committed fortunes to endeavors and poor men's sons to bloody battles. Byron struck a match to the end of the cigar, careful to ensure the burn was even. Then he looked up and continued. "And when he gave the spoon to the guard and didn't resist he showed consciousness of guilt. He had committed a crime, he was caught and he knew it. Ergo he was sane under the law." Byron struck a second match and held the end of the cigar over it, engulfing that which had not charred.

"How do you know he wasn't in some kind of trance?" Henry asked.

"That's the way he was when Henry met him," Mary offered.

"But that's not how the prison guards are gonna tell it at the trial," Byron said, and finally allowed himself one puff and then another, until the cigar was lit. He watched the smoke rise, blue-gray against the light up to the vaulted ceiling made of Arizona copper from the family's mine. "They'll say it was a typical convict revenge killing."

"But . . ." said Henry.

"Kid," said Byron, examining the cigar with satisfaction and seeing that all the tobacco was engaged in one glowing ember, "you asked for my advice so I'll give you the best legal advice you ever got. You go to trial, try to get the charge knocked down, get yourself some experience, show people you know how to cross-examine a witness and how to write an appeal, and don't make any enemies along the way, and for God's sake stop sounding like Eleanor Roosevelt."

He drew on the cigar once again, and the ember glowed brighter.

"She's not the worst person in the world to sound like," Henry said defensively.

"Yeah," said Byron, smiling, "but she's got even better connections than you have."

Henry let that one slide. He was determined not to let this degenerate into the Henry-and-Byron shows of his adolescence, especially not in front of Mary. It was one thing to be turned lovingly from a man into a boy by an older woman like Irene, it was quite another to be turned into a kid by your big brother. Besides, Henry told himself, a man's life was at stake after all, not to mention his first case.

"Byron, there are extenuating circumstances here. A man is put into the hole for three years. That's got to—"

Byron broke into his plea for compassion by pushing back from his desk and walking around to his little brother and planting a condescending pat upon his shoulder. "Henry," he said expansively, "I know you're a sucker for a cause, but this is not a demonstration at Harvard for world peace with the prep-school proletariat. These guys play hard ball. You've got to grow up, kid, and you've got to do it now." He let out a stream of the finest smoke that money could buy.

"Don't call me kid," said Henry. "Okay?"

That night, Mary and Henry walked along Fisherman's Wharf, eating the crab meat they'd bought from one of the outdoor vendors. There were Christmas decorations all over the place but the chill-to-the-bone fog was so thick you couldn't see them.

One of the great and vastly under appreciated advantages of wealth, Henry thought, is a warm overcoat. Thus he was able to enjoy his cracked crab and not feel the evening's chill.

"I can't remember my Dad except in court," he said to Mary who walked along beside him. He did not know what made him say it, and had he thought of it, the words would have been censored, would not have been allowed to escape his lips. Certainly not in so naked a form, nor so suddenly and without warning. They had, after all, spent the evening discussing the case, and for all his resentment of his brother, the talk had been of tactics, of matters legal and strategic, of importance only to one not only admitted to the bar, but equipped as well with his own client, and a federal Murder One at that. Thus, the jump to his father was more than awkward, it was revealing. Perhaps he could steer her gaze from his eyes to the court connection. Yes, that was it, of course, the connection was the law. The connection was a matter between attorneys. "Isn't that weird?" Henry said. "I used to sit in the courtroom and watch him. I was only about six years old but I remember, God, he was good. Nobody could cross-examine like that guy."

He took another bite of the crab meat and dipped it in the little paper cup of sauce and fed one to Mary and then continued, "He'd walk up, real friendly. Just plain folks, ya know? And he'd just sneak up on 'em and give 'em just enough rope to hang themselves with and then, *whap!* He'd spring the trap and down they'd go.

"Clarence Darrow congratulated him on some case. I mean, it was like my Dad was on a first-name basis with Jesus."

"And that's all you remember about your father?" Mary said, dabbing at the corner of her mouth with a napkin.

"He smelled like tobacco. His coat smelled like tobacco, I remember that," Henry said. Then realizing that that perhaps was too personal, created a door which could be opened into pain, he added, "He was a busy man."

"What about your mother?" Mary asked, and then linked her arm through Henry's.

"I was three when she died," he said. "I don't remember her. I think I remember her singing but maybe I just made it up."

Mary looked up at him. "So it's just been you and your brother?"

Henry pulled the Brooks Brothers overcoat closer around him and turned up the collar. "He was already grown," Henry said, pushing the collar up towards his cheeks and closing the coat across his chest. "So he was too old to, you know, be a buddy like a regular brother, and too young to be . . . to be a parent. He did what he thought was expected of him. He paid the bills and gave the lectures about why things were impossible. Just like today."

They were silent as they walked a few steps and then Mary said, "His advice wasn't all that bad, you know?"

"Wasn't it?" Henry replied, shaking his head with undisguised bitterness.

"No," said Mary, forcing Henry to look her in the eyes. "It wasn't."

That night, at home alone in his apartment, Henry replayed the evening and the day before him. He was a lawyer, it came down to that. It was what he had, perhaps the only thing that was truly his, that he could count on as his own, that was not given to him or handed down by virtue of his name, held in trust to be claimed at an appropriate age. Byron paid the bills, but Henry was a magna-cum-Harvard-laude, newly minted lawyer. You could pay for that education, but you couldn't buy it. And Mary, for as much as he wanted her, as much as he luxuriated in the warmth of Mary's arms around him, and lost himself inside her, Mary, too, was not his own. Nor could he ever be sure what she saw when she looked at him—a lover or a bronze nameplate on a thirty-story building. So he told himself, at the end of the day what you have is this, you are a lawyer, an officer of the court, licensed by the state of California to do legal battle on your client's behalf, and for this day right here and now, you are the only thing that stands between this person and state-appointed death. You're a lawyer. You've got a client. Defend him.

Chapter Six

HENRY WAS ESCORTED down the corridor by a new jailer. Had he paused to reflect upon it, it might have struck him as ironic that lawyers visiting jails regarded jailers as servants, or perhaps gas station or parking lot attendants, or at the very most, as doormen in rundown hotels, whereas the prisoners, on the other hand, regarded them as Gods. Willie was waiting at the cell door; not standing and staring but waiting, as if all he had to do in life was stand and wait for a visit from his friend. When the jailer opened the cell door, Willie motioned Henry in and stuck out his hand and said, "Hi, buddy. How are ya?"

Henry was taken aback at this change not just in attitude, but alertness. "Uh, hi, Willie," he said.

"Sit down," Willie said like a gracious host. But there was something more than grace here. It was almost like a lover trying to make up for a first spat. "Listen," Willie said, "You're not mad at me, are ya? About me blowin' up at ya the other day. I mean, you

don't talk to people for so long you forget how to do
it."

Henry broke into a smile, unable to believe his
ears. "You're talking!" he exclaimed. "Willie, you're
talking just like . . ."

"Yeah," said Willie nodding his head and smiling,
as if he could not believe the change which had come
over him either. "I been talking to everybody. Like I
can't shut up now, you know? I been shaking people's
hands, too. I like it. Say, you're not mad, though, are
ya?"

"No, Willie," Henry said smiling and shaking his
head like one might at the incessant prattlings of a
precocious child. "I'm not mad."

" 'Cause I'll get the hang of it," said Willie without
missing a beat. "I mean, I got a sense of humor, you
know. An' you an' me, we'll have some good times
before it's over. You know how to play cards?" he
said and sat down on the cot next to Henry as if ready
for a game.

But Henry for his part had already put his briefcase on the cot between them and extracted his legal
pad and fountain pen. As excited as Willie was at
newfound speech, camaraderie, and intercourse with
fellow man, and specifically with a kid of his own age
with which to talk and joke and play and gossip, so
Henry was equally filled with excitement at the pros-
pect of finally getting down to business with his client
and beginning his defense. Finally, he had a client
who could talk.

"Willie," said Henry, ready to begin the crusade.
"Was there any light at all in the cell where you spent
three years?"

"It's like when you offered me that cigarette," Willie said.

"Willie," said Henry, who had the beginnings of a notion in his mind, not so much a legal point as an emotional pitch, a piece of bait with which to hook a jury. "I want to get this straight, okay? This might be important."

But Willie was already happily re-living their past repartee. "You offered me the cigarette and I said, 'That shit'll kill ya.' Pretty good, huh?" said Willie, chuckling to himself at the memory.

"Willie . . ." Henry tried again.

"That shit'll kill ya, see?" Willie repeated. "That was the funny part. You don't think that's funny?"

Willie waited for a reply.

Henry tapped his pen.

"Willie, you've got to help me if I'm going to defend you," Henry said.

"Yeah, sure," said Willie.

Henry paused long enough, he hoped, for Willie's mind to take the new tack. Not just of the question, but of the matter at hand, which was, after all, their mutual dedication to his defense at trial, to doing everything humanly possible to give Henry the weapons he needed with which to battle Bill McNeil. The starting point was obvious. "Did you kill this man Avery Clark?" Henry asked.

Willie nodded his head up and down, up and down. "I must have," he said. "I'm here. I don't remember it, but everybody saw me so, you know . . . Sure."

Henry wrote the reply word for word into his notes and then looked up. "But you don't remember it?" he asked.

"Uh, no. But so what?"

So what indeed, thought Henry. *You did it, you don't remember it. There's got to be something one can do with that. People may not remember what they had for lunch a week ago last Tuesday, but they remember if they've murdered. They remember if they've ripped somebody's throat out with a spoon. Sane people remember such things, ladies and gentlemen of the jury. Sane people whose capacities are not diminished remember . . .*

"Did you *want* to kill this man Avery Clark?" Henry asked and waited with pen poised above the paper, hoping the answer that would be forthcoming would be no, definitely no, one hundred percent, positively no. I didn't mean to do it, I never thought of doing it. I looked up and there the spoon was in my hand as if it acted of its own accord but it wasn't me that did it.

"Sure," said Willie good naturedly, "I wanted to kill the snitch."

"But you didn't plan it, did you?" Henry asked. *He didn't plan it, ladies and gentlemen of the jury. It wasn't premeditated. There was no premeditation. The death penalty cannot apply here since there was no premeditation. One does not plan a murder with a spoon handle.* "You didn't plan it, isn't that correct?" Henry asked.

"Sure I did," said Willie, smiling. "Every day. It's all I thought about somewhere after the first year. I started thinking about it, how I'd kill whoever it was. That saved my life."

That saved his life! Henry shouted to the jury in his mind. *It was self-defense! He did it to save his life! Tell them, Willie, tell them!*

"That and baseball games and jerkin' off," Willie said in a matter-of-fact, friendly way that was downright cheerful. "I did times tables for a long time. That helped. Go ahead, ask me anything. A hundred and forty-two times ninety-three. Go ahead, ask me that one."

Henry all but threw up his arms in defeat, as he contemplated the effect that Willie's masturbation would have upon the jury. He had to find a way to reel this fruitcake back in. "Clark was a snitch," Henry said, "And he was the reason you landed in the hole for three years. How long after you came up out of the hole—"

"Thirteen thousand two hundred and six," Willie said, cutting him off.

Henry was completely lost. He stopped writing and looked up. "Thirteen thousand two hundred," he said. "What . . . what are you talking about?"

Willie smiled beatifically with unmistakable pride. "That's the answer," he said, "A hundred and forty-two times ninety-three. Go ahead, figure it out. That's the answer. I can do that all day long."

"Willie," said Henry, fighting with all his might at his own exasperation and growing resentment that the gods had given him this lunatic to defend. "Please try to concentrate on what I'm saying."

"I know what you're saying," said Willie, offended both at the lack of appreciation for his mathematical accomplishments and the inference that he was a lunatic incapable of understanding a direct question. The point was, he had been sharing and that which he had wanted to share had been ignored, if not declined. "I know what you're saying," he repeated.

"How long was it?" asked Henry once again.

"I don't know, okay?" Willie said, turning away from him and searching through a pile of newspapers Henry had left behind. "I don't remember. What . . . what's this new girl I seen in the papers? This Ingrid Berger. She some kinda looker, huh? You seen any of her movies?"

"Willie," said Henry, snatching the papers away, "I want you to think, goddamn it!"

"I don't want to think!" Willie shouted, clutching at his skull as if it was splitting apart. "I spent three years in the goddamn dark smellin' my own shit and piss, doin' nothin' but thinkin'. I hate thinkin'. I can't think!" Willie all but collapsed down into the cot, holding his head in his hands, rocking back and forth, back and forth.

"I can't sleep," he said, "Every time I close my eyes I'm back in there an' it's all black. I'm fuckin' crazy!" He looked up at Henry, his one good eye blazing. "I want to talk about what I want to talk about an' you keep askin' me these dumb-assed questions!"

And then he broke down crying, sobbing uncontrollably, weeping like a child. Henry crossed over slowly to him and tentatively put his arm around Willie's shoulder and held him as he cried. As he did so, there was one of those fleeting shadow memories that flitted like a moth across the screen where movies of his childhood played out inside his mind. It was someone rocking him sometime when he cried.

"I'm sorry, Willie," he said, holding Willie to him and rocking him gently, trying to remember if this was the way he had ever been rocked, "I'm . . . I'm just tryin' to help." Had someone ever said that to him? Had someone ever rocked him, saying, Henry, I'm just trying to help. Was that the tone of voice, was that the way it felt? And then Henry felt a pulling at himself as if his conscience were trying to get his attention, as if someone was threatening a swift kick in the butt, saying, Get your mind back on business, he's your client, this is your case, act like a lawyer. "I'm tryin' to save your life," he said, "But I can't do that without your help. Even . . . even if that means digging up some painful memories, ya know?"

Willie stopped crying. The tears stopped but not the sniffling that continued, Willie's head pressed tight against his shoulder. At least Henry thought he was sniffling and then realized Willie was sniffing instead. Sniffing at his jacket. Well what the hell was that all about?

"You okay, buddy?" he asked, leerily, almost laughing at himself in his thoughts. *Okay? Did I just ask this certifiably insane homicidal maniac if he was okay?*

"What is this?" Willie said, and sniffed again at the tweed.

"What?"

Willie sniffed at Henry's jacket once again, seemingly following a trail. "This . . ." said Willie. He sniffed again and then recognized it. "That's perfume, ain't it?"

"Huh?" said Henry, pulling back a little, and having no idea what his killer client might do next.

"On your jacket," Willie said, not in the least bit threatening, but almost in a kind of awe, a reverence, with a definite sense of wonder, a peasant in the

midst of riches, a leper at a healer's convention.
"That's perfume ain't it?"

"I don't know," said Henry, awkwardly.

"I ain't sayin' you're queer," Willie said with great
deference, and then reverently: "You got a girlfriend,
right?"

"Well," said Henry, weighing what the psychic and
emotional cost of an affirmative response to that
question might be. "Yeah," he said, just dipping his
toe into those troubled waters.

"And she musta hugged ya," Willie went on, quietly, touching the jacket to his cheek, as if it were a
holy garment. "Pressed up real close to ya." He was
quiet, closing his eyes, breathing in what fumes still
lingered, deeply. "Could I, could you . . . take your
jacket off?" he said. "An', an' just let me smell it,
please? I forgot what that was. That's perfume, ain't
it?"

Henry slowly took his jacket off and gently handed
it to Willie, like it was a foreign article, one he had
never seen before, so unaware was he of the seemingly magical properties it possessed. "Here," he
said.

Willie held the jacket up close to him, rubbed it
against his cheek, softly, rocked it back and forth and
then closed his eyes and whispered, soft as a feather,
"What's she like?"

"Willie," said Henry, bending down close to him,
"I'll make you a deal, okay? I'll tell you one story
about movies or girls or sports and you tell me one
memory about somethin' I ask you about. Deal?"

Willie opened his eyes, unable to believe his good
fortune. It was as if he had found a lamp worthless,

discarded and forgotten by one and all, only to touch it, rub it, believe in it and have the magic genie appear and say, to you, O Master, I grant this wish. Give me but one worthless memory and I will give you rubies, girls and sports. "Yeah, sure," said Willie.

"Okay," said Henry. "Now . . ."

"I never been with a girl," Willie said quietly, "you know? I never even kissed one. But I remember perfume. I remember the way it smelled."

The Public Defender's office was all decked out for Christmas. There was the sickly tree that was to Christmas trees what rickets-ridden dwarves were to Clark Gable. There were the latkes on the plate that Liebowitz brought in and the won tons put there by Charlie Woo. There was the mistletoe tacked as a joke above her office door and the sign she had put beneath it, reading, OUT-OF ORDER. There was everything that had been there last year and the year before and the year before that as well. The only thing that wasn't there was any sign of Henry. Mary had not seen him in three days. She poked her head into Henry's office and saw no sign of recent habitation. Then she ran into Leibowitz, the other junior lawyer, down the hall.

He looked her up and down as he always did. It was an unconscious habit, an involuntary response to the sight of her and smell of her. Liebowitz had asked her out before Henry had arrived upon the scene and Mary's response was a firm refusal, no fraternizing with co-workers, especially of the subordinate variety.

"That's what she says to me," Liebowitz had told

the hang-around-the-urinal crowd. "And two weeks later, she's schtupping Baby Warbucks."

"Leibowitz," Mary said, disregarding his once-over. "You seen Henry? He hasn't been here for days."

"It's Christmas Eve," he answered, grabbing his coat and muffler. "Maybe he went out of town." As for Liebowitz, he was on his way to a party at the DA's.

Prosecutors, it was his experience, gave much better parties, the booze was better and the atmosphere manic in its abandon, as if those whose lot in life it was to hold people to the law felt they were entitled to flaunt the mores of an admittedly puritanical society, at least once a year, on the birthday of the Savior. Defense attorneys on the other hand, never completely lost their missionary caste. Moreover where McCasslin was concerned, Liebowitz was convinced it was entirely within the realm of possibility that she would have the audacity to assign him some bullshit task on Christmas Eve, thinking that as a member of the tribe, he did not observe the yearly party rituals. Thus, Liebowitz made for the exit as quickly and unobtrusively as he could.

Mary caught him by the sleeve before he could make good his escape. "He was supposed to be with me tonight," she said, and then aware as she always was of the men's room gossip, she remembered to add, pro forma, "to prepare the diminished-capacity plea."

Normally Liebowitz would have relished the opportunity for a sarcastic if not necessarily snappy comeback. But there was the party at the DA's to consider, and so he assumed the most air he could muster under the circumstances. "He did say somethin' about workin' on his case," Leibowitz said.

In Henry's apartment, the phone rang and rang and rang but there was no answer. It was the fourth time Mary had called, and she imagined any number of possible scenarios at the other end of that ringing line. He was ill. He was out. He was dead. He was with another woman. He was dead. She saw each mental picture, each in its turn, saw it as clearly as a crime-scene photo; the empty room, the cadaverous body, the bimbo in the bed. In all probability she knew he was not there and anything she was imagining should have had a different setting. He was in a hospital and he was ill. He was in a morgue and he was dead. He was in a motel room with the bimbo and she would kill him. Then he would be in the morgue and he'd be dead. But with no place else to look, Mary decided to drive over to his flat and torment herself there in his apartment.

Henry's building was a lovely turn-of-the-century example of post-earthquake Victorian architecture, complete with bay windows that afforded a wonderful view of the Golden Gate Bridge and, beyond it, Alcatraz.

The superintendent of the building, a Chinese gentleman named Chan, was dressed as Santa Claus as he led Mary up the stairs.

"Lady," he said, "it's Christmas morning. This better be some kinda emergency, I'm on my way to a party."

Going up the stairs, Mary reflected on the number

of practitioners of other religions who never seemed
to miss the Christmas party whereas Methodists like
herself . . .

Inside the apartment, all the windows were open
and the air was freezing.

"Jesus," said Santa Chan, "it's like an icebox in
here. What is this guy, some kinda fresh-air nut?"

Mary went over and started closing the windows.
For his part, Chan figured he had done all that could
be expected of him. He watched Mary shut the windows and as unobtrusively as possibly, he sniffed the
air for corpses. Truth be told, he knew little of Henry
and cared less, but a corpse was a corpse and if there
was one here in this apartment there was no way he
would be attending any paries before New Year's.
Thus taking her turned back as a kind of tacit dis-
missal, with a parting, "Ho, ho, ho," he was gone.

"He never leaves his windows open," Mary said to
Chan until she realized that Chan was gone. Then
called out, "Henry!"

She wished the Chinese Santa had stayed. To steel
herself, she visualized Henry's body lying in the
kitchen, bloodied in the bathroom, stuffed into a
closet. It was a morbid habit, that much was true, and
she would have had difficulty explaining it to anyone.
But it was an oddly comforting thing, she thought. It
allowed herself never to be caught off guard, always
to be prepared. For nothing could ever be worse than
that which she had already imagined, even if it were
only a split second before. It was a survival technique
and it had never failed her.

Her visualizations completed, Mary looked into
the tiny kitchen. There was no one there. She went

over to the bathroom door. It was closed. She opened it slowly, fearful for some reason of what she might find. She looked in. There, huddled up in the corner, in his underwear, with a three-day growth of beard, was Henry.

There was a black blanket over the window, which was obviously open because she could see the wind pushing against it. Henry looked up, squinting against the light, shivering against the cold.

"Henry!" Mary said, rushing toward him. "My God! Are you all right?"

"I'm so cold," he said, huddling in against her.

"What happened?" Mary said, trying to help him up and keep him warm at the same time. "It's freezing in here."

"I been in here three days."

"Let's get you out of here," she said, leading him toward the door.

"No," Henry said, pulling away from her. "I want you to feel it, to feel what it's like. To feel what it was like for Willie."

He closed the door plunging them into darkness.

"Henry," Mary said, frightened, "please, let's get out of here. You're like ice."

Henry looked crazy, clinging to her. "I been so cold," he said like a homeless child. "And . . . it's scary. God, it's scary in the dark. I'd lay here and think about what it musta been like for him, and then I didn't care what it was like for him and all I'd think about was you and how all I wanted was to be warm and—"

"Henry," Mary said, putting her arm around him

and leading him once again toward the door, "let's get out of . . ."

But when she looked at him, there in the crack of light that crept into the room, there was a fierceness in his eyes that she had never seen before.

"I opened the window," he said, "and blocked out the light and laid on the floor, trying to get the slightest notion of what it was like for Willie. Except I chose to do it and he didn't. That's the difference. They did it to him," he said. "I know how to defend him now, Mary. I know how to defend my client."

Chapter Seven

On THE MOST IMPORTANT morning thus far in Henry Davidson's life, the morning on which he was to make his opening statement in the trial of the *People* vs. *Moore*, the morning he had trained for, prayed for and waited for longingly like an orphan waits for adoption, on that morning of mornings, he had the hiccups.

These were not the mild burp-into-your-napkin variety. These were hiccups that could shatter glass. These were the ones that wracked the chest, convulsed the body, dipped, and then kicked back like a case of whiplash. These were tubercular hiccups. Spastic hiccups. Volcanic hiccups.

Mary found him in the consultation room off the second floor of the old Federal Court Building. There he was in the very room once used by Darrow and Brandeis, bent over at the waist trying to drink a glass of water upside down from the wrong side of the rim, the water sloshing over the rim and his shirt and tie as he gulped it down. He waited for the hiccups to stop and then looked up at 'Mary and said, "Okay, it worked. Let's go."

Then he hiccupped.

The bailiff poked his head in a second later and said, "Mr. Davidson, Judge Clawson is ready to enter the courtroom and he said to tell you he's not going to wait for you any longer."

"No problem," Henry said and hiccupped. The bailiff left, shaking his head.

"Damn it," Henry grimaced. "Do you believe this? I got a guy's life in my hands, resting on my ability to communicate and I've got the—" He hiccupped once more. "What else is going to go wrong today?" he said.

Mary took his hand and then took a deep breath as if finally deciding to unburden herself.

"Well, I wasn't going to say anything," she said, "but now that you mention it, you're not the only one who's having a rough day. And mine's a little worse than hiccups."

Henry hiccupped. As far as he was concerned, nothing could be worse.

"What?" said Henry, challenging the list of possible human miseries.

"No," Mary said. "Forget it. You've got enough on your mind. I'll tell you later." She turned away, but Henry took her arm.

"What?" said Henry, "Come on Mary, Jesus, you know how I hate it when—"

"I'm pregnant," Mary said.

There was a long silence. It was broken by Henry.

"Oh, my God," he said. "Oh, my God. Oh, Jesus.

Oh, not now, why now? I mean, are you serious, you're pregnant?"

"No," Mary said, smiling, "but it cured your hiccups, didn't it?"

"All rise," said the bailiff. The courtroom was more than half empty, just a few crime reporters with nothing better to do and the usual crones who wandered in off the street to kill a few hours, witnessing a life-and-death struggle carried out in pleasant, dark-wooded surroundings. Here and there were faces right out of the French Revolution.

Some of them would have been at home sitting beneath the guillotine knitting hair. Some of them would have felt at ease watching lions gnaw on Christian bones or gladiators killing one another with sword or lance. These were those for whom the courtroom presented the last great free-of-charge form of public entertainment. It was justice as a blood sport. They collected assaults like stamp collectors hoarded numbered plate blocks. They categorized aggravated rapes like butterfly collectors tacking new-found specimens out on labeled cards readied for glass cases. They gathered crimes like miser coin collectors and traded them amongst themselves, reminisced about the best, the rarest, the bloodiest, the ones with real appeal. And for all of them, the *crème de la crème,* the flawless crystal cat's-eye, the most prized of all wax dummies in their grand Guignol collections was the pre-meditated murder of one person by another. Though to the real connoisseur, this one lacked a certain *je ne sais quois.* There was no white-skinned bludgeoned damsel, no

jealous lover, no inheritance or insurance, no juicy
older woman/younger man, no society status, nor any
real tabloid potential. This, all in all, was even less
than a run-of-the-mill mugging. It was a prisoner of
all things, who had killed another prisoner. Well,
what else did they have to do with their time and who
cared, when all was said and done, what they did with
one another? One more, one less. . . . It was all the
same since they were themselves inside already anyway. Out of sight, out of mind, and all of that. Still,
San Francisco in December was an awfully cold place
to spend a day out on the streets and inside the
courtroom was indisputably warm. And then there
were the crime reporters. Amongst them was one
particularly grizzled old newspaperman by the name
of Hoolihan, who chewed perpetually on an unlit
spit-soaked cigar as he worked the racing forms.

Willie, for his part, seemed bored by the goings-on.
He played with the baseball cards Henry had given
him and was about to stick a square of bubble gum
into his mouth when Henry slapped his hand. Just
then there was a bit of a stir at the back of the room.
Henry turned to see Warden Humson and Mr. Glenn
enter the court as the prosecutor, McNeil, worked
the jury like a holy-rolling circuit preacher about to
beat Satan back and win new converts to the Lord.

"And so, ladies and gentlemen of the jury," Mc-
Neil said, leaning on the rail, looking each of them in
the eye, impressing upon them one and all, individually and as a group, that they were society's last wall
between chaos and salvation, "the prosecution will
prove beyond the shadow of a doubt that the defen-

dant Willie Moore did, on the morning of December fifteenth, kill Avery Charles Clark."

McNeil crossed away from the jury and stepped toward Willie, speaking in a voice full of moral condemnation. "That he did so in a cold-blooded, cowardly fashion. That the murder was premeditated and that it was a grisly and particularly brutal crime." Here, he turned back to the jury and lowered his voice. "Even in a world of hardened criminals, a world of brutal men, this murder stands out for its barbarism. The prosecution will call witness after witness who saw this grisly deed committed in front of their horror-stricken eyes. I will apologize now for what you will be forced to hear."

It was at this mention of promised atrocities that a brief but palpable stir swept through those gathered in the room. There was a tingle if not a shudder that you could feel. The Madame LaFarge-types at the back whispered greedily to one another, imagining aloud the bloody tales they felt for sure would liven up a dull proceeding.

"But," said McNeil, "it is your duty to hear it as jurors, and perhaps, too, it will make your job easier. For the United States of America, which is the plaintiff here . . ." And when he said it you could almost hear the drum rolls, see the fireworks and Old Glory snapping to and fro above the ballparks, snapping in the wind. "The United States of America," McNeil intoned as if he and it were one and the same, "will demand that you return a verdict of guilty of murder in the first degree so that this . . . animal," McNeil turned and pointed at Willie, "will receive the punishment commanded by the Bible, an eye for an eye

. . . a life for a life." McNeil let the Bible sit out
there in front of them, paused and let it slowly trans-
form itself into a vaporous Old-Testament, desert-rat,
Sistine-Chapel, sinewy-finger-pointing God of righteous wrath and indignation who commanded, not
suggested, nor proposed, but commanded on pain of
exclusion from salvation of the sulphurous burning of
eternal souls that the forfeiture of life be answered
with the forfeiture of life. McNeil was not a prosecutor, he was in fact their prophet standing there before
them as Elijah stood his ground before the pagans
and called down lightning from on high.

"You," he said, looking through their eyes and past
them down into their souls, "you will be able to return that verdict with a clean conscience, without the
slightest doubt or hesitation. For if ever there was a
man guilty of murder it is William Moore, and if ever
there was a man who deserved to die for that most
heinous of all crimes, it is the accused who sits before
you. It is *that* man. It is William Moore and it is your
duty to find him guilty as charged and recommend
that he should die."

The jury all but shouted amen as McNeil walked
back to the prosecution table and threw Henry a little
look that all but said, What do you think of them
apples, kid? From the back of the courtroom, Mr.
Glenn smiled and Warden Humson checked his
watch. As far as one and all seemed to be concerned,
the trial was over before it had begun. What was
there, after all, to say? What could anyone say to
dispute the facts?

Willie Moore was a convict.

Willie Moore was an incorrigible housed in the

world's most escape-proof prison built to protect society from fiends who could not be rehabilitated by a civilized society.

Willie Moore killed Avery Charles Clark.

He planned it.

He did it.

He must die for it.

If they skipped lunch, they could probably wrap it up today. It was nine to nothing in the bottom of the ninth and the smart money was leaving the stands.

Even Clawson suppressed a yawn as he turned to Henry and said, "Mr. Davidson. Are you ready to make your opening statement at this time?"

Henry took a deep breath, uttered a silent entreaty to the merciful God of hiccups and said, "Yes, Your Honor."

Henry looked at the jury, then at McNeil who pulled back a lip into his crocodile smile. He looked out into the courtroom and saw Mary nod encouragement just as Irene and Byron walked in and took their seats in the back. He looked at his client on trial for his life, who was looking not at his attorney, but at his Joe DiMaggio rookie trading card.

"Your Honor," Henry said, and as he said it he thought, *Now it's real.* This was not for the imagined memoirs nor to impress his girlfriend nor prove a point to his brother, this was not turning cartwheels on the lawn for Irene's applause. This was not a demonstration to an admired or despised professor, nor the winning of a bet, nor the taking of a dare, nor a debate, nor moot trial, nor moot anything. This was real and when it was over a verdict would be read.

Judgment would be passed and if McNeil had his way, Willie would be dead.

It was everything he'd hoped for.

. And now it was everything he feared.

"Ladies and gentlemen of the jury," he said, and felt himself go lightheaded, sway back onto his heels, reach out and grab the table and bring his feet back down onto the floor.

"This is my first case. I've never tried one before. And here it is. The great moment I've been waiting for. All my life, this is all I've ever wanted to do. I didn't have the same kind of heroes as other kids, Babe Ruth or Lou Gehrig or Jack Dempsey," he said, looking at Willie. "My hero was and is Clarence Darrow ′ . . . Emile Zola . . . and when I was a little kid in my fantasies I would see myself standing, just like I am now, before a jury of twelve good men and true where I would plead the case of an innocent man who's been unjustly accused."

Henry put his hands firmly down against the wood of the rail that stood between the jury and the court. He took a long, deep breath and knew in two more sentences there would be no turning back. He would have jumped in with Willie on his back, chained together and they would sink or swim and Willie would live or die depending on whether or not he could pull it off.

"And here it is," Henry said. "Here I am and here you are, just like I remember it from when I was a kid. The only problem is . . ." Henry paused again for effect. He looked at Willie, then back at the jury and said, "He did it! Can you believe that? My first case, the one I've been waitin' for, and the guy I'm supposed to defend—did it. He killed the guy! I can't tell you he didn't, because he did. I know it. The prosecutor knows it, Willie Moore doesn't know it exactly, 'cause he can't remember it, but he won't deny that he did it. All those witnesses the prosecutor said he is going to call will tell you so. Willie Moore killed Avery Clark and we all know it, and now you know it, too. So what are we all gonna do here for the next few days or weeks? Now that we all know, why don't we just save the taxpayers a lot of time and money and find the guy guilty as charged right here and now and send him up to San Quentin and gas him?"

Henry took a step away from them, looked at the jury not as individuals but as a blur, afraid almost to look them in the eyes. He looked up at Clawson who looked at him as if he'd only just then landed on the planet Earth, a visitor from Mars. He looked at McNeil who smiled encouragingly as if to say, I'm on your side now, kid. Go get 'em.

"That's what we all know is going to happen anyway," Henry said. "That's what Willie thinks. I can't even get him to help me fight for his life. All he wants to do is have a friend to talk to till the state kills him." He looked at Willie and Willie smiled back up at him, relieved that Henry finally got it.

"The prosecutor knows that's what we're going to do," said Henry. "Just take a look at him," he said, pointing at McNeil. "He looks like the cat that ate the canary."

McNeil made a gracious little nod of the head in Henry's direction which caused a snicker or two to roll up from the jury box.

"My boss knows that's what we're gonna do," said
Henry. "That's why he okayed assigning a first-time
lawyer like me to a federal murder case, 'cause he
knows it's a lost cause anyway. A monkey could try it.
That's what he told me."

There was open laughter now, and one thing more
as well. Slowly, inexorably, snicker by snicker and
laugh by laugh, they were beginning to like Henry
Davidson, and more than relishing his newfound
popularity, Henry realized he had taken the first step,
he had gotten them to forget McNeil's Old Testament wrath. They were not on his side, not by a long
shot, but they were listening.

Henry leaned in as if letting them in on gossip, as if
opening a family album, pointing to a picture and
saying, That's my Uncle Harry, that's my Aunt Cla-
rice, this is me at Christmas. He had to make himself
into their little brother, he had to change the face of
the killer into that of a boy.

"My brother," he said, just as folksy in his delivery
as anything his father had ever done, "my brother
who, I gotta tell ya, is a big-time corporate lawyer,
slick as they come. He knows that's what we're going
to do. And my fiancée, well, I do believe she knows it
too." He had even let them see his girlfriend. They
didn't teach this at Harvard, they taught it at the
freak show. The carney pitch man dressed as Clarence Darrow trying to be as likeable as Tom Sawyer,
as their neighbor's kids, as their nephews, one of
them and not the enemy.

"There's only one problem that's gonna keep us
from wrapping this thing up in record time," he said
with a Huck Finn twinkle in his eye. "The problem

is," he all but whispered, "Willie Moore did not act alone. They did not catch all the killers."

Henry paused and turned away and the courtroom started to buzz. It was electric. He could feel it. He could feel the jurors lean forward behind his back, lean in towards him, crane their necks and cock their ears to get in early on the secret. And all the time Henry was fishing for just one juror who would buy it, sniff it, nibble around it, take a bite and wind up with a hook in cheek that snagged him on the lure of reasonable doubt, and hang the jury instead of his client.

Now Henry loved it.

Now there was nowhere else he'd rather be but here. Nothing else he'd rather do than this, what he had trained for, what he had hoped for, what was his not by rights divine, but by genetic disposition and the best education that money could buy.

They were with him now. He was leading, they were following, and the real toe dancing could now begin.

"There was," Henry said, "a co-conspirator. An evil, vicious, monstrous co-conspirator who took Willie Moore and placed him in a psychological coma, so that he was incapable of doing anything *but* killing Avery Clark!"

Henry looked over at McNeil, whose mouth was wide open, caught completely unawares.

Henry crossed over to the jury box, looking from one juror to the next, seeing them now for the first time as individuals.

There was the one with glasses, who looked like an accountant.

There was the mustached one with hair slicked back who looked like a movie gangster.

There was the one Henry thought of now as the insurance salesman.

There was the one who looked like a leader.

There was the one who looked like a follower.

Which one? Henry thought. *Which one of you is gonna hang? Which one of you is gonna ride with me all the way down to the end of the line, look his fellows in the eyes and say, "Not guilty?"*

"Willie Moore," said Henry, "was the gun, but the real murderer is this co-conspirator who held the psychological gun in a steel grasp, loaded it, and pulled the mental trigger. And it is because of this co-conspirator, whom we shall name in this courtroom, that Willie Moore is *innocent.*" Henry let the word hang there in the air, where before there'd been a wrathful God in search of vengeance. "Innocent of the crime of murder."

Henry turned and walked back to the defense table, as McNeil jumped to his feet.

"Your Honor," McNeil said, indignantly, "I must protest!"

"Kinda figured you would," Clawson replied with a slight smile.

"Your Honor," said McNeil, "I am aware that this is counsel's first case, and perhaps we shouldn't expect too much, but this is absurd! I would ask Your Honor to direct counsel to produce some evidence, some proof that such a co-conspirator exists, before allowing him to waste the court's time with this line of defense." McNeil turned and glared at Henry.

"Mr. Davidson," said Clawson, "can you bring forward some proof of the existence of a co-conspirator?"

Henry rose. "Not at this time, Your Honor," he said, "But it is my intention to offer such proof during the course of the trial."

McNeil turned back to the judge.

"He can't offer any proof," he said, "because there isn't any!" He pointed at Willie and little flecks of spittle appeared white on his lower lip. He wore the same look that flashed across his face in the squash game, slamming home a point like a sadistic cop cracking skulls at a low-life bar. "This man," he said, pointing at Willie, "spent three years in solitary confinement, three years during which time no one had any influence over him, because no one had any contact with him. He came into the dining hall, asked one convict one question. That convict spoke one sentence to him, Your Honor. That is hardly enough to put a man into a psychological coma!" He let out a derisive laugh and one of the jurors smiled appreciatively.

Henry looked at the juror and put a mental pin right between his beady eyes. The notion of anything psychological to this member was a mountain the size of the Himalayas which Henry would have to scale. But at this stage of the game he wasn't worried about identifying the one juror he *couldn't* convince. He was just hoping to find at least one that he could. Right now, it was just throw it all up there and hope something sticks to somebody, just one.

Clawson interrupted Henry's ruminations, saying, "I'm inclined to agree with the prosecution, young man," he said. "Unless you can show some basis for that line of defense, I will sustain the prosecution's objection."

And then Henry thought, *Whap, there goes the trap, Dad.* And for that instant he could see him, see him clearly in his mind just as he had looked in this very courtroom staring up at him from barely more than kneecap level, his father turning, winking at the boy when the trap clanged shut. Henry turned and it occurred to him for the tiniest moment that there was no one watching who would appreciate his wink.

"Your Honor," Henry said, looking up to the judge, "the District Attorney, with his own words, has just made my case for me."

"That'll be the day, Sonny," McNeil said with the look of a schoolyard bully who's just been invited to fight behind the gym. It was the look that said, You want to fight me, punk? I'm gonna kick your ass. His eyes held Henry's but Henry didn't blink, not first and not at all. Instead, he turned slowly to the judge and listened as his own voice rolled out across the court.

"Your Honor," Henry said, fire blazing in his voice now, "for three long, tortuous years, no one and nothing had any influence over Willie Moore whatsoever. No one and nothing but Alcatraz! He went into that dungeon a petty criminal who had never harmed or attempted to harm another human being in his entire life." He turned and looked at the jurors and pointing to Willie, said, his voice dropping low, "And he came out a vicious, barbaric, maniacal murderer. A man who had been put into a kind of psychological coma." He looked the sneerer right in the eyes as if daring him to laugh now.

"Within an hour of coming out of that hellhole, he did what would have been unthinkable to him only three years before. His only thought . . . was murder. His only impulse . . . was murder. His first act . . . was murder! He was himself a murder weapon, but the hand that held the weapon and plunged it into Avery Clark's throat belonged to someone else!" He had them now. He didn't know if they were going to go all the way with him or get off at the next stop, but for right now each and every one of them sitting there, eyes riveted to his, was on board. He had dreamed of this. He had dreamed exactly this. He strode the length of the jury box, looking from them to the judge and back again like the hottest Pentecostal evangelist who'd ever pranced upon a pulpit, promising brimstone or salvation, damning sinners and saving souls, and in tent meeting parlance it would have been said, he had the spirit. When Henry spoke again he imagined himself not in church but standing before a legion of men of which he was now a part, a living tableaux of warriors walking bloodied but unbowed, banners streaming through clouds of cannon smoke, an army of those who had spent their lives and fortunes battling injustice.

"Forty years ago," Henry began again, slow and low and building it all anew, "a man named Dreyfus was on trial. And forty years ago Emile Zola stood before a French courtroom and pointed with the finger of justice at the conspiracy of the General Staff of the Army of the Republic of France. So, too, do I now stand before you and this jury and say that the conspirators are present in this courtroom today!"

And as he turned Henry envied every European

barrister who was allowed to wear a robe. He wanted
to see the folds of cloth swirl and his hand snake out
from beneath the magician's sleeves. He wanted to
hear the pop of cloth and hiss of hem whirling as he
turned and pointed to the back of the courtroom and
said in a voice he hoped was full of history that reso-
nated with the cries of shackled men in darkened
dungeons screaming innocence to an unhearing
world and praying to the god who had forsaken them
to send one down to earth who would stand for them
and bellow for all to see and hear, *J'accuse.*

"I point . . ." Henry said, the white cuff shooting
out from beneath his sleeve and the outstretched
pointed finger aimed like a duelling pistol straight at
their hearts, "I point to the associate warden Mr.
Glenn," and their eyes swung with his arm straight at
the jailer. "I point to the warden Mr. Humson."
Their eyes obeyed and zeroed in on the engineer.
And then Henry turned to take them in with his look,
and swung them all with his arm that arced through
the room, straight to the window and through it, to
the mist shrouded in the bay, the Rock that sat there
breaking through the fog and said, "And I point to
the institution known as Alcatraz and say, *I accuse!*"
There was an audible gasp that echoed around the
room. "I accuse them collectively and individually. I
accuse Alcatraz of the murder of Avery Clark! I accuse Alcatraz of the torture of Willie Moore! I accuse
Alcatraz of practices more fitting to the Spanish Inquisition than the United States of America! I accuse
Alcatraz of something even more heinous than the
murder of one man."

He turned and faced Humson and Glenn, then

turned back to the jury, about to take them along on a journey none of them had bargained for. "I accuse the warden and associate warden and the institution known as Alcatraz of crimes against humanity! Willie Moore will not be the only defendant here. Alcatraz is on trial!"

The courtroom went nuts. Reporters who had sat like hags at a hanging waiting for the door to spring and rope to snap jumped up from seats, slamming into one another, grabbing lapels and pushing rivals fishing for coins in pockets and stumbling over briefcases as they ran headlong for the bank of phones that lined the halls. McNeil leapt up, turning in his chair and banging his knee against the prosecution's table leg, stifling a grunted mumbled, ow-shit-son-of-a-bitch-bastard, then straightening and shouting at the top of his lungs as the judge attacked the little circle of wood with his gavel as if it were a cockroach that would not die.

"Your Honor, I object!" McNeil shouted, spittle flying now from off his lips in a crescent trajectory that hit the court reporter squarely in the eye. "I object, Your Honor!" he shouted.

"So do I," mumbled the court reporter, wiping the back of her hand across her eye and staring daggers at McNeil.

Clawson went after the cockroach again with his little wooden hammer. "This courtroom will come to order!" he bellowed red-faced, jowls shaking, shouting above the din. "This court will come to order!"

The gavel was impotent against the chaos and Clawson turned to the courtroom cop and for a moment it looked as if his intent were to issue orders to fire point-blank into the revelers. "Bailiff!" he shouted. "I will instruct the bailiff to clear the court if order is not restored!"

Order, however, was out the window, down the toilet, had left the barn and flown the coop and otherwise departed from the courtroom.

So His Honor did the only prudent thing he could in the given circumstances and still give the appearance at least of one who is in control. "This court," Clawson declared, "is in recess until nine o'clock Monday morning!" He took one more ineffectual swat at the wooden disk and beat a hasty retreat to his chambers.

"Your Honor, I object!" McNeil shouted like a wounded soldier being abandoned to the enemy. "I object," he shouted to the closing chamber doors and then mumbled *sotto voce,* "Fucking coward."

For his part, Byron was already out the door shaking his head, toting his alligator briefcase and checking his watch while mentally shaping up excuses for his impending late arrival. Irene, however, was still there, matronly and reassuring in her presence. She turned to Mary and smiled ruefully. "He finally found himself a cause," she said.

Just then Humson and Glenn pushed past them, elbows out, heads ducked down and shoulders hunched as they dodged those reporters who had not already raced for the phones.

"I have no comment at this time," said Humson to his shirt buttons.

"Get out of our way," Glenn said, his hand reaching instinctively back for the blackjack at his hip. He wished he could use it on just a few of them.

Willie Moore turned to Henry with a quizzical look. He hadn't the vaguest notion of anything that had transpired and as the bailiff led him away he waved to Henry and said, "You got time for some cards?"

Before Henry could even consider an answer to Willie's generous offer, McNeil grabbed Henry by the arm and hissed, "If you pick up your foot, counselor, you'll see you just stepped on your dick."

Outside, in the corridor, there was a line of phone booths jammed with reporters who had appeared out of nowhere, like vultures circling a fresh kill, abandoning other trials when they heard the commotion.

"Here's your headline," one of them shouted into the receiver, "Alcatraz On Trial!" And it echoed down the hall bringing more reporters still to circle this exotic bait.

Another reporter who had heard only snatches of Henry's statement was already dictating his story over the phone. "The veil of secrecy which has shrouded Alcatraz like the morning fog promises to be lifted at last," he said, sneaking a peek at another reporter's notes, "as the defense accuses the Rock of crimes against humanity and the warden declares no comment to charges of torture . . ."

In the men's room Henry was standing at the urinal as Hoolihan stepped up next to him, his notebook out and in hand. "Mind if I ask you a few questions, counselor?"

"Mind if I take a leak?" Henry said.

"Can I quote ya?" Hoolihan replied, chomping on his cigar.

Henry looked at him, not knowing if he was serious or kidding.

"You got a lot to learn, kid," said the newsman. "Never give a reporter a line like that. Hoolihan. *Tribune.*"

"I know who you are," Henry said, standing there relieving himself as he realized he was in the midst of giving his first interview.

"Well don't bother shakin'," said Hoolihan. "You got your hands full. You an' me are gonna make a deal, kid. You need me."

Henry flushed the urinal and turned to face him. "Really?"

"Yeah. You go up against Alcatraz, you make yourself a lot of enemies."

"Like who?" said Henry, as he crossed over to the sink.

Hoolihan just smiled.

"J. Edgar Hoover, for one," he said. "Justice Department, for another. Hell, you can't get money for a Ten Most Wanted List unless you got an escape-proof place to keep 'em, an' it can't be escape-proof unless everybody who tries to escape dies. That's probably why they stuck your boy in the hole for three years, except he didn't die, so now they're gonna make sure he does."

Henry dried his hands and looked Hoolihan up and down. There was something so obviously vulgar about the man that he appeared to have nothing to hide. "You said something about a deal."

Hoolihan removed his cigar and spit a fleck of tobacco from his tongue. "I'm the only nationally syndicated columnist in this city," he said. "You think

Clawson isn't gonna get a few phone calls from Washington this weekend? You just stepped in a ten-foot deep pile o' shit an' I'm the only guy with a rope."

He paused for a second and let that one sink in and seemed to take Henry's measure in a glance and then went on.

"I can give you leads in two hundred and fifty newspapers across the country. And that's just what it's gonna take for Clawson to look at McNeil and say, objection overruled. You can put Alcatraz on trial, kid. It's up to you." Hoolihan stuck his cigar back in the corner of his mouth.

Henry knew that he was right. He knew that Clawson's ruling would have less to do with the rule of law and legal opinions handed down by appellate courts than with the court of public opinion. Whatever pressure was brought to bear against the judge from one side had to be balanced, indeed outweighed by pressure brought to bear by the other, namely Henry's side. A syndicated column in two hundred fifty newspapers was an awfully big stick. "I'm listening, Mr. Hoolihan," Henry said.

Hoolihan leaned in close enough for Henry to smell the whiskey, the cigar, and the marinara stain on Hoolihan's jacket. "I get exclusives," said Hoolihan. "You don't talk to anybody before you talk to me. Your client doesn't talk to anybody *but* me."

"Suppose I say yes," Henry said. "How do I know—"

Hoolihan cut him off. "Kid, if Joan of Arc woulda had me in her corner, she'd have been king of France instead of a weenie roast."

Chapter Eight

"YOU GO TO HELL," Willie said. He was flipping baseball cards inside his cell when Henry brought the whole thing up again. His one good eye blazed out indignation. Henry was asking him to violate every rule of his existence, all the basic tenants to which citizens of the penal countryside subscribed. To do so was the equivalent of asking a cloistered monk to volunteer for excommunication. Willie didn't understand how anybody could be so stupid!

"Willie," Henry said, "you're the one who's gonna die if I can't get some corroboration about the conditions at Alcatraz. I need names! Names of guys who'll come and testify about what goes on over there."

He had taken out the yellow legal pad to take down the list of names and Willie had all but smacked it out of his hand.

"Mr. Glenn sees you talkin' to 'em an' they go straight to the hole," said Willie, unconsciously touching the scar that ran from just above his eye almost to his chin. "He'll kick the shit out of 'em to make sure they don't talk."

"I can get a court order to make them testify!" said Henry.

Willie jumped to his feet. The stupidity of it was more than he could take sitting down. This guy didn't understand anything.

"Yeah, an' what's your court order gonna do for 'em when they're back on the Rock, huh? Glenn'll kill 'em. That's what! An' you want me to finger 'em for ya?"

"Willie," Henry said quietly, "It's the only chance you've got. It's your life, damn it!"

Willie turned to him and spoke what for him was the most obvious truth in the world. "Hank, I ain't *got* a chance. They're gonna kill me anyway so who needs this shit." He scratched his head and let out a laugh. "I mean I don't even know what you're talkin' about up there."

"I'm talkin' about justice," Henry said. It was the right word, he thought. He could have talked about career or childhood dreams. He could have talked of college ideals and proven his bona fides by citing the numbers of workers' rights demonstrations in which he had participated. It wasn't as if he hadn't been willing to risk academic probation by marching in favor of the losing side in Spain. It wasn't as if he hadn't donated money for the wounded of the Lincoln Brigade. But being in the hole for three years, Willie's familiarity with those in the forefront of the fight against global fascism might be wanting. So he summed it all up in a word anyone could understand, especially a prisoner. He was talking about justice.

Speeches, Willie thought. *Talk an' speeches.* He gathered up his cards. "Hank," he said, "I don't got an education but I'm not stupid. I killed him, they saw it and they're gonna kill me. It's as simple as that and nothin' that you can say is gonna make it any different. So I don't know what you got to get so excited about."

Willie shuffled the cards twice and put them on the cot between them for Henry to cut, but Henry just shook his head.

"This trial doesn't mean anything to you? Doesn't interest you even?" he asked.

"Well," said Willie, still waiting for him to cut the deck, "you look like you're havin' a good time doin' it so, you know, I don't care. I mean, main thing to me is I got somebody my age to talk to till they gas me. Cut 'em," he said, tapping the deck.

"I don't want to just play cards with you or flip baseball pictures up against the wall! I don't want to just talk to you about baseball and girls, okay?"

"Why not? Isn't that what friends do? Shoot the shit? Have fun?"

"Willie," Henry said, "I'm not your friend. I'm your attorney and I'm trying to save your life!"

Willie pulled the deck of cards back towards him. He felt sadder than he could remember. "Yeah," he said, "Well, I had attorneys before, but I ain't never had a friend. I had a sister. I ain't seen her since I went to jail the first time."

And it was then for the first time that Henry could remember that he watched a great devastating wave of sadness seem to wash over Willie Moore. It changed his features, puffed his eyes, puckered out his lip, reddened the scar that carved a jagged line across his face, stooped his shoulders, bent him as if from the weight of ages of grief. "I got nothin' and nobody. I don't need a lawyer. I need a friend. This whole thing you're doin' is one big jerk-off, so you can prove somethin' to some guy named Zola or something. But you're not doin' it for me. So if you want to do something for me, let's just play cards."

He put the deck back in front of Henry defiantly.

"Play solitaire, Willie. I got a case to try," Henry said and got up to leave.

"Go on then," Willie said to the back of Henry's head. "You don't know anything about baseball, you won't play cards, you won't talk about girls. What the fuck good are you?"

What the fuck good are you? was a sentiment regarding Henry which was shared evidently by Henry's boss, Lou Henkin, who was waving a sheaf of papers in Henry's face and shouting, "What the hell do you think you're doing with this think?!"

"Mr. Henkin," said Henry, doubly embarrassed to have this happening in front of Mary, "I'm tryin' to defend my client! I thought that's what we're here to do."

"Then defend him, for Christ's sake," Henkin said. "Try an' get the charge knocked down. Show it was a crime of passion!"

He looked over to Mary for some kind of support. Maybe she could talk some sense into him.

"There wasn't any passion," she said dryly. "He just walked over and ripped the guy's throat out with a spoon handle."

Wonderful, Henkin thought, *wonderful.* Then he whirled on Henry again. "Go figure out how you're gonna cross-examine McNeil's witnesses, instead of this psychological coma crap that doesn't mean anything in a court of law."

"Well, I think it does, Mr. Henkin," Henry said, standing. "And as long as this is my case—"

"Fair enough," said Henkin, turning his back on them both. "I tried to talk reasonably but you're not goin' for it so it's not your case anymore. Done!"

He reached for the door handle when Henry said, "Mr. Henkin, they're printing my opening statement in two hundred and fifty newspapers all across this country." Henkin stopped in his tracks.

And Henry thought, *It worked.* Everything Hoolihan said was true and everything Henry had been instinctively smart enough to grab at was vindicated. He watched it happening in Henkin's eyes and one of life's great truths began to unveil itself before him like a stripper peeling yet another layer. What motivated most men was not greed, nor lust for power, not ambition, nor any drive toward any given goal. It was fear, and the direction in which it always led was to the rear. The histories of men's lives retreated from event to event, from confrontation to escape, from escape to cornered rat. Then some would fight and some would surrender and you had damned well better know which was which.

Henry leaned in toward his boss. "You want to be the one to pull me off this because you're afraid of taking on Alcatraz, that's fine," he said. "But I'll tell my side of it to Jerry Hoolihan. You want to play hard ball? I'll play hard ball."

When Henkin turned around it was with the expression and air of a Dutch uncle whose nephew is blackmailing him. "I'm tryin' to be your friend, Henry," he said, putting his arm around his subordinate. "You know who the warden of Alcatraz is? He's the most highly respected warden in this country, dealing with the world's hardest criminals! You try and make Humson look like a Nazi and they will eat you for breakfast!"

Henry stayed expressionless, so Henkin turned to Mary. He *hated* being nice to anyone, let alone underlings.

"And if you have any concern for your boyfriend here, and your own career, you'll make him see the light!" he said, and slammed out of the room.

It was then that it occurred to Henry that he was not quite sure which of them was cornered.

After dealing with Henkin, Henry figured Alcatraz couldn't be much worse.

He was wrong.

There are places on earth whose appearances are deceptive. Not Alcatraz. It looked like what it was, America's Devil's Island. But then the French had already done away with their Devil's Island. So that left only Alcatraz. It sat there in the fog, looming up out of the darkness with a visage that reminded Henry of all the books he'd read about the Chateau d'If and the Count of Monte Cristo.

He would not have been in the least surprised to come face to face with the Man in the Iron Mask in a place like this. The only difference was the Man in the Iron Mask and the Count of Monte Cristo were imprisoned in a penal system which had been in disrepute for over a hundred years. But in this year of 1941, no prison in America had more clout than the place which held Al Capone, the Rock from which no man left alive before his time was up.

Henry and Mary had been ushered up the metal stairs to Mr. Glenn's office. They had demanded to see Warden Humson.

"Mr. Humson's not here," Glenn said, leaning back in his chair.

"Well," said Henry, trying to be affable, "we don't really need him, though that would have been nice. What we do need is to talk with those prisoners who saw the killing."

Glenn looked him up and down. It was the kind of look he reserved for new prisoners who were reported to be wise guys.

It was a look which said, I'll break you, a look which promised violence, a look which whispered in your ear no matter who you were on the outside, all that is over now; I can take you, strip you, soak you, beat you, gouge out eyes or sear your flesh and not only is there nothing you can do to stop it, there is none who will even hear your cries, there is no one who is not afraid of me, no one who does not do my bidding. It was a look that said, I am Dracula, I bid you welcome.

"Not possible," Glenn said, softly, barely moving his lips.

"Really, why is that?" said Henry, as pleasantly as he possibly could to hide the very real fear he felt despite himself.

" 'Cause I said so," Glenn said, and then he said nothing else, just stared into Henry's eyes.

Finally Henry broke the silence as he felt sweat run down his back, though the room was cold as a crypt. "Mr. Glenn, I am an officer of the court here to interview potential witnesses. You interfere with that and you'll have to appear in federal court Monday morning to show cause."

Glenn sat looking at him, rocking back and forth, saying nothing, just smiling the most terrifying smile Henry had ever seen. It was the smile of a man whose work was torture and it was a smile of a man who loved his work.

Within an hour, Henry and Mary found themselves seated opposite a man named Barkdoll, in the visitation area. They were separated from him by bullet-proof glass and they spoke through a phone.

"Mr. Barkdoll," Henry said, "I'd like to ask you a few questions."

"What's in it for me?" said Barkdoll.

"Uh," Henry said, "I'm not sure I understand."

"What do I get for talkin' to you?" Barkdoll asked.

Mary spoke into her phone. "Did you see Willie Moore kill Avery Clark, Mr. Barkdoll?"

Barkdoll looked her over without changing expressions.

"Why should I talk to you? What are you gonna do for me?"

"Mr. Barkdoll," Henry said, leaning forward, speaking he hoped like a man making a serious offer, "I'll be frank with you. I don't really care if you saw Willie Moore kill Avery Clark or not. I want to call prisoners to the stand who will testify about life on

Alcatraz. About what it's like to be in solitary, about the beatings, about meals every three days. About light deprivation and being thrown into solitary without any clothes or blankets. I know what's going on here. I want a jury to know that, too."

Henry knew there was no way Barkdoll could turn him down. He was here after all to champion their cause, stand up for their rights.

"Tell 'em to get caught robbin' a bank, they'll find out," Barkdoll said dryly.

"All we want you to do is take the stand and tell the truth about what it's like here," Mary said.

Barkdoll would help. He was, after all, one of the men for whom Henry had stood there in the court with the outstretched hand and pointed finger of justice crying out for those who could not speak, there will be justice for all, for prisoner and for jailer. Barkdoll would help because he had seen that Mary and Henry cared. They were people who cared. People willing to stand up and be counted for the things in which they believed. Barkdoll would help because these things were good.

"What do you think I am," Barkdoll asked, "a chump? I ain't gonna do shit for you 'cause you can't do shit for me. You can't get me no good time knocked off. You can't get me no privileges. You can't even get me seconds for dessert. I testify for anybody, I testify for the DA. He's got some juice here. Not you two. Hell, I'll lie for him . . ."

The next prisoner they interviewed was a man named Stevens. He was huge, hairy, and covered with tattoos. He made both Henry and Mary thankful for

the bulletproof glass between them. His conversation
was short to the point of eloquence.

"Fuck you," he said.

"Mr. Stevens," said Henry. "Did Mr. Glenn tell
you not to cooperate with me?"

"Fuck you," Stevens said.

"Do you know that I can get a writ of habeas
corpus testificandum that will force you to appear in
court and testify?" said Henry.

"Fuck you," said Stevens.

"A man's life may depend on your testimony."

"Fuck *him*," said Stevens.

"Thanks for your time, Mr. Stevens," Henry said.

"Don't mention it," said Stevens. "Oh, and
you . . ." He looked at Mary. "I'd *like* to fuck you."

When he was gone, Mary said, "I think it's time for
Plan B."

Glenn was in his office. His phone buzzed and he
picked it up. "Yeah, send 'em in," he said into the
receiver.

Henry and Mary came in and Glenn didn't bother
to offer them a seat. He rocked back and forth in his
chair, his pencil tapping against his teeth, tracking a
fly with his eyes as it buzzed, stopped, buzzed, flew,
stopped again, and then quick as a frog's tongue he
darted out a swatter that splattered the fly into a
purple blotch across the wall. He turned from Henry
and Mary to his intercom. His words were so softly
spoken and so few in number neither of the two
young lawyers could make out what had been said.
Then the door opened behind them, a trustee prisoner came in with a tissue and carefully wiped the fly
off of the wall. This man Henry recognized as one

who had been just a year before one of the most
feared killers in the country. Now he was a eunuch.
As the trustee left the room, Glenn turned to Henry
and Mary. "Well, counselors," he said and smiled,
"has your day been a fruitful one?"

"It's not over yet," said Henry. "I'd like to see the
solitary confinement cells. Specifically, I'd like to see
the cell where Willie Moore was held for three
years."

"Too bad," Glenn said, jutting out his jaw. "That's
off limits."

Henry and Mary both looked crestfallen.

"But—" said Mary.

"Off limits," Glenn repeated.

Mary looked at Henry to see if he had any further
ideas. "Off limits," he said, shrugging.

Mary stuck out her hand to Glenn. "Well," she
said, "thanks for your time."

He reached out to shake her hand, but before he
could do anything, Henry smacked a set of papers in
his palm as hard and decisively as Glenn had swatted
to death the fly.

"What is this?" Glenn demanded.

"You've just been served with papers, Mr. Glenn,"
Mary said. "That is a court order instructing you to
permit us access to the solitary confinement cells and
to allow me to take pictures of same, to be used as
exhibits in the trial of the *People* versus *Moore*. You
are also instructed to hand over to us the complete
medical and disciplinary files listed therein. If you
refuse to do so you will be in violation of a federal
court order and will have to appear in court to answer for same. Have a nice day."

They were accompanied down to the dungeons by a guard who watched them like a hawk. He was there to strictly prohibit any contact between them and any of the inmates in solitary. Then Mary faked a fainting spell. Henry told the guard that Mary needed air and the guard told him he was instructed not to leave them alone.

"Now look," said Henry. "She needs air and I need to finish taking these pictures. We don't have any keys and we've already been searched for files and whatever else you think we might be carrying. We're not going to spring anybody, if that's what you're afraid of."

"All right, all right," the guard said warily, and took Mary under the arm and brought her up the metal stairs out of the punishment block. That's when Henry turned to the closed doors of the dungeons and said, "My name is Henry Davidson. I'm Willie Moore's attorney. I can force them to let you out and come to San Francisco and testify in court. You'll be given lunch in the Federal Court Building's cafeteria and dessert. Just give me your names. Do that for me and I can do what I said for you."

Henry showed up the next day in Willie's cell with a piece of paper on which were written three names of men who would testify in return for a promise of federal cafeteria peach cobbler.

"I don't get it," Willie said, looking at the names.

"What don't you get?" said Henry.

Willie looked at the names on the paper as if they made up some sort of riddle.

"Why would these guys agree to come and testify? What's in it for them?" Willie asked.

"Does somethin' have to be in it for them?" Henry said.

"Sure. That's why it don't smell right."

Henry took the paper back and put it in his brief-case.

"Maybe you have a few friends you didn't know about, Willie," he said.

"Maybe," Willie said, "But not these guys. I don't even know these guys."

"Well, maybe they just care, huh?"

"Care about what?" said Willie. "You're not makin' any sense."

Henry snapped the briefcase shut and turned on Willie. "Care about changing things, care about that word I mentioned to you before," he said. "Maybe they care about injustice, maybe they have the guts to do what you won't do: stand up and be counted. Hell, they're willing to do it for a stranger. You're not even willing to do it to help yourself. When are you gonna get involved in this case?"

It was a learning experience, Henry thought. This was the first time in his admittedly short life that he had met someone for whom great thoughts and high ideals were simply not in their repertoire even as clichés. Heretofore they were at least that . . . at the very least comfortable clichés which served as common points of reference to be paid at the very, very least the lip service which was their due in every circle of which he had been a part. Willie was outside the circle and it was disconcerting.

Willie just smiled good-naturedly. "Hank, for a

smart guy, you're awful slow," he said, leaning back on his cot and putting his feet up on the bedstead. "I'm dead. I keep tellin' you that. You can't change Alcatraz and there ain't no justice. I don't know why it's like that. It just is. So why fight it?"

Chapter Nine

MONDAY MORNING AT NINE o'clock precisely, Judge Clawson banged his gavel and addressed the court. Both Henry and McNeil sat with pencils poised above legal pads, listening attentively for his ruling, while Willie sat arranging baseball cards by club and year.

"Before I hand down my ruling on Mr. McNeil's objection," said the judge turning to Henry, "I would like to address a few words to counsel for the defense."

Henry squirmed in his chair. He was about to get dressed down by a federal judge and he knew it. The only question would be whether it was a perfunctory admonition to cover Clawson's own ass, or whether it was the equivalent of the executioner asking if your neck was nice and comfy on the block. Henry gulped audibly so that McNeil turned, looked at him, and smiled, confident that his adversary was about to go down in flames.

"Mr. Davidson," Clawson said, "you are hereby

put on notice that this court will not tolerate defense
counsel's using his position as an officer of the court
to further any political agendas which defense counsel may harbor."

He was leaning over the bench now, pointing the
handle of the gavel at Henry in much the same way
as Henry imagined Willie must have held the spoon
before he stuck it to Avery Clark. This was it. He had
overplayed his hand and allowed himself to be taken
in by Hoolihan. He was about to be flushed down the
toilet. His career and Willie's life were about to swirl
down the great crapper of federal jurisprudence.

"My decisions," Clawson went on, "on the admissi-
bility or inadmissibility of testimony and/or exhibits
will be governed solely by the rules of evidence, and
in each case their pertinence to the matter now pending before this court will be my only consideration. Is
that clear, Mr. Davidson?"

Henry in spite of himself, gulped again and sounding like a miscreant student who knew he was about
to be bounced out of yet another school, he nodded
and said, "Yes, Your Honor." Now it was coming.
Now he would turn to McNeil, the good son to
Henry's wicked one, and say objection sustained, pat
McNeil on the head, bounce him on his knee, give
him a candy and say, Go get 'em, sonny boy, eat 'em
up alive.

But instead and much to Henry's dismay, Clawson
was not finished with him yet.

"This court," he said, "will not be swayed by news-
paper headlines, and I would admonish counsel that
his attempts to try this case in the press and not before this court will put him in the utmost peril." He

paused a long time and poked the air with the gavel handle once again, and now spoke in his most threatening tones. "I will not hesitate to use my powers." And when he said powers, he hit the "P" as hard as he could, to let you know he had plenty. "I will not hesitate to use my powers to find counsel in contempt if I feel counsel is abusing his privileges. Is *that* clear, Mr. Davidson?"

It was even worse than Henry thought. He was not only going to sustain McNeil's objection, but sentence Henry for contempt as well.

Henry's contemplative self-pity was interrupted by Clawson saying, "Is that clear, Mr. Davidson, or is it not?"

"I think he's talkin' to you," Willie said, poking Henry.

"I know who he's talking to," Henry whispered to Willie. Then he looked up at the judge and said, "Yes, Your Honor. Very clear."

"Very well," said Clawson. "Prosecution's objection is overruled."

Overruled! Henry thought. He overruled McNeil? *He came down on my side?* Choruses should swell, shooting stars streak across the sky, rainbows should appear miraculously over Alcatraz with little bluebirds flying overhead!

"Exception," McNeil said through gritted teeth.

"Noted," said Clawson. Then he turned to Henry. "Mr. Davidson, you may pursue your line of defense regarding the Federal Penitentiary at Alcatraz and I will rule on any objections on a point-by-point basis. Call your first witness, Mr. McNeil."

Henry didn't want them to call a first witness. He

wanted to end the trial right there and declare victory. Unfortunately, though, as Henry knew only too well, this was just a point, neither game nor match. But it was a victory nonetheless, so Henry turned to Willie and said, "We made it."

Willie looked as if he could care less.

"Try and contain your emotions, Willie, ya know?"

"Fuck you," said Willie. "I'm bored."

McNeil stood, having totally regained his composure and his combative edge. "The prosecution calls Terrence Swenson."

"Terrence Swenson," said the bailiff.

Swenson, a tall, distinguished-looking man with hair graying at the temples took the stand.

Son of a bitch looks like Gary Cooper, Henry thought. They could have sent to Central Casting for the perfect image of a lawman and Swenson would have gotten the part.

"Do you swear to tell the truth, the whole truth and nothing but the truth in the matter now pending before this court, so help you God?" asked the bailiff, extending a Bible towards Swenson.

Swenson put his hand most respectfully on the holy book and then turned and looked at the jury and said, with just a hint of a Southwest drawl, "I do."

"State your name for the record," said McNeil, approaching the witness.

"Terrence Martin Swenson."

"Mr. Swenson," said McNeil, reading from his notes for effect, "are you employed as an officer of the Federal Penitentiary at Alcatraz?"

"I am," Swenson said.

McNeil looked up from his notes at Swenson.

"Were you on duty in the dining hall on the afternoon of December fifteenth, 1940?"

"I was," came the reply.

"Will you tell the court what occurred on that day?" McNeil said, and stepped away from Swenson, so that the jury could get a good look at him and coincidentally, so that Henry's view of the witness was obstructed.

"Well," said Swenson, "I was on duty in the dining hall, and, uh, everything was normal, and I saw the defendant—"

"William Moore?" said McNeil, pointing at Willie.

"That's correct," Swenson said, looking first at Willie just to make sure. He was the perfect witness. Prosecution asked for surety and he gave him surety. He was dignified, articulate, and properly somber and he was about to put a rope around Willie's neck. "I saw him standing over Avery Clark. Moore lifted up his chin and plunged a metal object, which I later learned was a spoon handle, into Clark's throat, and, uh, he ripped it open. There was blood all over the place by the time I got there."

Henry snuck a look over in the direction of the jury, not wishing to appear too concerned. By the expressions on their faces and the looks they threw in Willie's direction, there was no doubt about the direction in which McNeil was leading them, and it had nothing to do with diminished capacity.

"Did the defendant appear to be ranting or raving?" asked McNeil, looking once again at Willie.

"No, sir," said Swenson.

"Was he frothing at the mouth, perhaps?" asked McNeil politely.

"No, sir," Swenson said.

"Did he at all give the impression of one who was insane?" McNeil queried.

Henry leapt to his feet so hard he almost threw his back out of joint. "Objection, Your Honor," he said, like a kid in class who finally knows the answer. "Witness is not a qualified psychiatrist as far as I know."

Clawson in an offhand way motioned for Henry to sit down. As far as the judge was concerned he got no points for this, even though he did say, "Sustained."

McNeil didn't look in the least perturbed. He had gotten exactly what he wanted in front of the jury.

"Did he appear to be in control of his actions?" asked McNeil. "Did he appear to know what he was doing?"

"Objection," said Henry, though less energetically.

"Sustained," said the judge, as if it were pro forma, which it was.

"What did you do," McNeil asked with obvious relish, "after you saw Moore, in your words, rip Clark's throat open?" McNeil even threw in a gesture of ripping open the victim's trachea.

"I rushed to disarm him," Swenson said, "I grabbed him, got him in a hammerlock."

"And did the defendant say anything to you?"

"No, sir," said Swenson.

"No argument?" asked McNeil. "No shouting? No yelling?"

"No, sir."

"So as far as you are concerned," McNeil said, turning to Henry, with just a hint of a smile, "as a correctional officer not a psychiatrist, but as a seasoned correctional officer, this was not a crime of passion, but a cool, calculated deliberate act?"

"Objection," Henry said.

This time Clawson intoned, "Overruled. You may answer the question."

"Yes, sir," said the Gary Cooper lookalike. "Moore did it just as cool as a cucumber."

"No further questions," McNeil said with a smirk to the defense table, and sat down.

Henry looked down at his notes and decided that the sooner this guy was off the stand, the better. "We have no questions of this witness at this time, Your Honor," he said, "but reserve the right to call him at a later date."

Next up was an elderly guard by the name of Blackmun. McNeil made a big deal about the fact that Blackmun had been a federal prison guard for over thirty years and Henry knew exactly where he was going with that.

"You've been an officer at Alcatraz from the first day it opened, is that correct Mr. Blackmun?"

"That is correct, sir."

Even though Blackmun was pushing sixty, he was still a powerfully built man. Unlike Swenson, who looked like a diplomat, Blackmun could have passed for a convict himself. That's why it was all the more effective when McNeil asked, "In all your years as a correctional officer, both at Alcatraz and before, in over three decades in fact, dealing day in and day out with the most hardened criminals in this country, have you ever seen a more brutal act of one man killing another . . ." McNeil paused and then moved out of the way so that the jurors could get an unobstructed view of Willie and then continued, ". . . than the bloody murder of Avery Clark by this defendant, Willie Moore?"

Blackmun took a breath and you could see that the horror of the memory was real. "No, sir," he said, "It was the most godawful thing I ever seen one man do to another and I'll remember it to the day I die."

"No further questions," McNeil said, and he was so pleased with himself, he almost pirouetted back to the prosecution table.

Henry stood and had he been the attorney that his father was, he would have taken a few minutes to warm up to the witness in front of the jury, to commiserate with him over what he had been forced to witness, to show that he was on this elderly gentleman's side. But they didn't teach that at Harvard. They taught aggressiveness and a kind of arrogance, as if being smart was all that counted in life. They taught you to win and right now Blackmun was in the way, an obstacle to victory.

"Mr. Blackmun," said Henry. "You testified that you have been a guard at Alcatraz for as long as it's been a federal penitentiary, correct?"

"That's right," said Blackmun, and the jury could see that he took offense to this smart-aleck kid's tone of voice. "Been a correctional officer longer than you've been alive."

"Great," said Henry. "And in all that time that you've been a correctional officer, longer in fact than I've been alive, to your knowledge, has a prisoner ever been held in solitary confinement for three years, with only thirty minutes of—"

"Objection!" McNeil said, springing to his feet.

"Sustained," said the judge, as Willie looked on and even waved a little to Blackmun, who smiled back at him.

"Your Honor," Henry said, crossing to the bench, "Mr. McNeil has made a big deal about this witness' professional experience. All I want to know is if in his professional experience he has ever—"

But now it was the judge who broke in. "Whether he's ever seen a prisoner in solitary for this length of time or the other," said Clawson, "is immaterial. Objection sustained."

Again, had Henry had the benefit of a few years of trial experience, he would have known better than to go at it again, because now he was not going against the witness or the prosecutor, but against the judge.

"Did you ever have occasion to know the defendant as a prisoner, prior to his having been put into solitary for three years—"

"Objection, Your Honor," said McNeil, who was really only giving his cues to the judge, who couldn't wait to say:

"Sustained, same rationale, Counselor."

"Same exception," Henry said, sticking his other foot in his mouth for good measure.

"Noted," said the judge.

But Henry would not leave ill enough alone. "Prior to the fifteenth of December, Mr. Blackmun, had it been your experience that the defendant was a violent prisoner?"

"Objection, Your Honor," McNeil said, faking exasperation with Henry's incompetence, doing a little show for the jury that said, Can you believe this kid, wasting *our* valuable time.

"The witness' experience with the defendant prior to the fifteenth of December," said McNeil, as if explaining this simplest fact of life to the most slow-witted child, "is not relevant to the witness' testimony on direct examination. If counsel wants to develop such testimony, let him do it on direct with his *own* witness and not mine."

"Sustained," said Clawson.

Henry looked over at McNeil who was sitting down and giving him the finger with the prosecution table hiding the gesture from the judge.

"No further questions," Henry said.

"We ain't doin' so hot, huh?" said Willie.

"How did you figure that one out," Henry said. "I thought you weren't paying attention."

"It just doesn't look like you're havin' too much fun," said Willie, and added hopefully, "You wanna stick of gum?"

At about that time, Mary McCasslin did not look like she was having much fun, either. She was sitting in Henkin's office opposite her boss, who held up a list of names on a piece of paper which he slid across the desk towards her.

"Where did Davidson get the three names on this list?" he demanded.

Mary looked down at the names and started to feel sick.

"Uhh . . . I don't know, Mr. Henkin," she said.

Henkin pulled the list back towards him and took a swig of the open bottle of Pepto-Bismol that sat on his desk. "These three men are all in solitary confinement," he said. "Henry gives the list to the DA as

witnesses he wants to call, and the DA asks how he
got the names. Glenn didn't give them to him."

"Maybe Mr. Moore did," Mary offered hopefully.

Henkin wiped the pink rim off his lips with the
back of his hand. "And maybe you faked a little fainting spell so your boyfriend could talk to prisoners
behind the guard's back. How stupid can you two
get?" He came around from behind the desk and
now stood looking down at Mary. "You think you can
trust those cons? They're smart enough to look out
for their own interests. They told Glenn that your
boy Henry said he could get them out of solitary if
they'd agree to testify for the defense and lie on the
stand. He even threw in a little free lunch if the lies
were big enough."

"That's not true!" Mary said, standing up herself,
ready to go toe to toe with her boss. "All Henry
wanted was to find one convict who would—"

"Jesus, Mary," said Henkin blowing up in her face,
"I—it's goddamn bribery. It's prejudicing witnesses.
Inducing testimony." He took a step away from her
and then turned back, wagging his finger in her face.
"It's conduct that can get him disbarred and you
along with him! Glenn and Humson are howling
mad. The DA's after scalps. The only question is"—
Henkin paused and brought his voice down to the
tone that meant a deadly threat, not for show, but for
real—"are you gonna let him take you down with
him? Because that's the only choice you've got Mary,
if you want to stay a lawyer in this state, that's the
only choice you've got. Trust me on that."

* * *

Dr. Harrison Kiley was on the stand. He was a slight
man with a pinched nose and thinning hair which he
combed forward in an effort to conceal a hairline in
full retreat. It made him look like an anorexic Ger-
trude Stein, a tubercular Roman emperor. He had
the sallow complexion of a convict, but then they all
did, Henry noted, everyone who lived on that island,
prisoner or jailer, they all had the same look and the
same complexion.

"Doctor Kiley," said McNeil, "you are the prison
doctor at Alcatraz, are you not?"

"I am," said Kiley, as if defending something of
which he was ashamed.

"And you are also trained in psychiatry, is that
true?" the prosecutor asked.

"That is correct," the doctor said. "Part of my duties in the U.S. Army—"

Here McNeil broke in, helpfully, "Where you at-
tained the rank of major?"

Kiley nodded his head up and down, emphatically.
"That's right," he said. "Part of my duties as a Major
in the U.S. Army Medical Corps involved psychiatric
work, counseling, treatment, what have you."

McNeil turned from the witness and looked at
Henry. It was the kind of look one could imagine
Babe Ruth had worn, pointing to the bleachers, a
look that said, Watch me pal, I'm about to knock this
one out of the park.

"Do you know the legal definition of insanity, doctor?" McNeil asked.

"Yes," the doctor said. "It is the ability to distin-
guish right from wrong."

"In your professional opinion, then," McNeil

enunciated each word, "as a medical doctor and based upon your years of experience in psychiatry and psychology, was the defendant, William Moore, legally sane at the time that he killed Avery Clark?"

Every member of the jury looked at Kiley. Henry had staked his case on a kind of mental incompetence and here was a qualified expert to slap his hand and say no. No way, no how.

"It is my considered judgement that the defendant, William Moore, was sane at that time," Kiley said, with such piety that you half expected him to add, And may God have mercy on his soul.

"Your witness," said McNeil.

Henry stood and crossed to the witness stand. "Doctor Kiley," he began, "were you called in to treat the defendant after the stabbing incident?"

"No," said Kiley, "I was not."

"Why?" asked Henry.

"It was not considered necessary," said the Doctor.

"By whom?"

"By the appropriate authority," Kiley said.

"By that you mean, Mr. Glenn . . . Mr. Humson? What appropriate authority?"

"Objection," said McNeil. "It's irrelevant. All we need to know is that it wasn't necessary."

"Sustained," said the judge.

Fine, thought Henry. *You close one door I'll open another.* He was gonna get this guy and this time they wouldn't stop him. "How are you usually called in to treat a prisoner?" he asked.

"Objection, Your Honor," McNeil said, putting more of an edge on his tone as well. "The practices and procedures under which Doctor Kiley is or is not called into a case are not the issue here."

"Your Honor," said Henry, "they are precisely at issue here if—"

Clawson turned on Henry as if he was getting a ruler ready for the youngster's knuckles. "Objection sustained," he said. "It is not the purpose of this trial, counsel's opening statement notwithstanding, to determine anything other than the innocence or guilt of the defendant."

There *it is,* Henry thought, *the son of a bitch got forced into ruling in my favor because of Hoolihan's articles.* And now he was going to make him pay for it. He'd given Henry just enough rope to hang both himself and his client.

"The witness," Clawson continued, "is the prison doctor, and he has already testified that in his expert opinion, the defendant was legally sane."

Henry turned back to Kiley. "Doctor Kiley," he said, "did you have occasion to speak with the defendant after the stabbing incident?"

"Objection," said McNeil.

Henry turned to the judge, not combative this time, but appealing to basic logic. "Your Honor, how can we know if Doctor Kiley's diagnosis—if you want to call it that—was valid, if we don't even know if he spoke with the defendant after the incident?" Henry held his breath, trying to look as innocent as possible. The judge could give him this one. This one was harmless enough, wasn't it?

They looked at each other like a couple of poker players, trying to decide whose hand was a bluff.

"Overruled," said Clawson. "Witness will answer the question."

In Henry's mind, he popped a tiny bottle of champagne.

"I did not speak with him," said the Doctor.

"Then on what basis did you arrive at the conclusion that the defendant was sane at the time of the stabbing?" Henry asked in a reasonable enough tone.

"By evaluating the reports of the witnesses and by my observation," the doctor said in the tone that doctors get when lay people question their diagnoses.

"You mean," said Henry, "you looked through a tiny peephole into a pitch black cell and on that basis—"

"Objection," said McNeil, with some urgency, sensing that Henry could inflict some damage here. "The witness has already answered the question."

"Sustained," Clawson said.

No problem, thought Henry. He put his hand on the witness box, trying to seem to be at least a little folksy instead of the arrogant prick he knew he was. "Let me see if I understand this," he said. "You listened to what the witnesses said, you observed the defendant, but you never asked him a question, never spoke to him?"

"That is correct."

"Did you feel that was sufficient in your professional opinion?" Henry asked, in what he hoped was his least confrontational tone.

"Objection."

"Sustained."

Shit, thought Henry. "Did you not want to talk to

Willie Moore?" Henry asked the doctor, "out of professional curiosity if nothing else."

"Objection," said McNeil.

To hell with it, thought Henry, *I'll get this in one way or the other.* "Did you not ask to interview him and were you not denied permission to interview him by Mr. Glenn?"

"Objection, Your Honor!" McNeil shouted and damn near stamped his foot.

"Sustained," said Clawson and then turned his full force on Henry. "Counselor, you will not ask another question until I have ruled on the first objection. Objection sustained, the witness is instructed not to answer the question, and the question will be stricken."

Henry turned to Kiley. "Did you ask permission of anyone to interview—"

"Objection."

"Sustained."

"Doctor," asked Henry, "you are currently undertaking a study of some sort at Alcatraz, are you not?"

Kiley looked around to see if someone would object and it was obvious that he wished they would. This was not something he wanted to discuss, but no one else saw the importance of it and so he was left out there, hanging. "I am," said Kiley.

"Is it your field of study to examine men at Alcatraz for nervous conditions? Are you an examiner in psychiatry studying the needs of men in confinement, their food and light needs?"

Now McNeil got it and got it but good. "Objection," he said, approaching the bench. "It's immaterial, Your Honor."

"Your Honor," said Henry, "the witness is carrying

out studies on prisoners," he raised his voice to make sure the jury could hear, "using them for laboratory mice to determine the effects of food and light deprivation on the human mind. I'd like to know—"

Clawson banged his gavel hard enough to send a spike through a railroad tie. "Objection sustained!" he said, the blood vessels in his temples pounding. He shook his gavel at Henry and said, "Counsel's last remarks will be stricken. The jury is instructed to disregard counsel's last comments. Counselor, if you have any further questions of this witness that are germane to the issue and to his testimony under direct examination, then ask them. If not, excuse the witness. If not, be prepared to spend the evening in the city jail, for I will find you in contempt, sir."

"Witness is excused," said Henry.

"Court is adjourned until nine o'clock tomorrow morning," Clawson said, banging the gavel.

And as McNeil packed his briefcase, he looked up at Henry and said, "You ought to be the poster boy for mercy killings, Henry."

That night, Henry and Mary were grabbing a late dinner at Alioto's. Henry was working on his notes for the next day's cross-examination while Mary glanced through the transcript of that day's proceedings. She shook her head occasionally. Finally, Henry looked up and said, "I wasn't too spectacular today, huh?"

"I don't know why you say that," Mary said. "You only managed to alienate the judge and the jury."

"I think the bailiff likes me," Henry said.

Mary reached across and took Henry's hand. "You're blowing it, my darling."

"It'll turn around when I get our witnesses on the stand," said Henry. He took another spoonful of the chowder that sat in front of him. It was cold.

"You mean the three from solitary," Mary said. "You can't trust them, Henry."

"They'll talk. They'll be only too happy to talk."

Mary looked out the window, not that there was anything to be seen except the fog. Then she took a deep breath and said, "They've already talked."

Henry looked up at her.

"To Mr. Glenn," Mary went on. "They said you offered to get them out of solitary in exchange for perjured testimony."

"Bullshit! Who said that?" said Henry. He pulled out his briefcase and started going through it for the list of convicts. His mind was racing for solutions. It's what his mind was trained to do, what he had trained it to do with academic disciplines all his life. Problem, then solution. There was a symmetry to life which was bound up in his Harvard youthful attitude. There was no problem to which there was not a solution. You just had to work hard enough to find it. And so he tore now through his briefcase, for lists, for proofs, for arguments and counter-arguments, and then Mary's voice broke through.

"Oh, Henry, if you stick them on the stand they'll say enough to get you disbarred." She looked down at the table and then back up at him. "They don't care, Henry. Don't you see that? The cons don't care. Willie was right. None of them care. So what's the use?"

Henry stopped going through the briefcase. "What are you saying?" he said.

By now Mary was fighting back tears. She blew her nose and then said, "Henry, withdraw from the case. Claim illness, claim personal problems, claim—"

"No!" said Henry, slamming his fist into the table and sending a perfectly good glass of Chianti flying. He took his napkin to mop it up when Mary took his hand and said, "Henry, you can either withdraw, or Henkin will pull you off, and if you try and go to Hoolihan he'll get the DA to show you tried to prejudice witnesses. You don't have any choice, my darling."

"You better believe I have a choice," said Henry who stood up and threw money on the table to cover the check. If she was going to side with them, that was fine with him. She either had confidence in him or she did not. "I resign," Henry said. "You're my superior. Consider that a formal resignation. I'll handle the case privately."

Henry was torn between wanting to leave and wanting her to reach out and stop him from leaving.

She didn't reach out, just looked up at him and said, "Oh, Henry . . . Why do you have to make it be like this? Why can't you just take the out they're offering you, instead of . . ."

Henry bent down to her, looked her in the eye so she would understand that this wasn't ego, it was principle. "Because it's my job and Willie Moore is my client!"

"Not anymore," she said quietly.

He stopped cold and spoke barely above a whisper. "What?" he said.

"He's already been notified that Henkin wants you off the case."

"Willie'll never go for it," Henry said defiantly.

Mary stared at what was left of her chopped salad, as if the secret of life and salvation lay there somewhere, behind the olives and the garbanzo beans. "He's already met the person who's been assigned the case and he's accepted new counsel."

The trap door sprang out from beneath his feet and he plummeted now down and down, knowing that it would come to an end when the rope snapped taut and broke his neck. It was just a question of how much rope was left.

"Who did he meet with? Who's the two-bit-asskissing son of a bitch who met with my client behind my back? Charley Woo, Leibowitz, who?"

"Me," Mary said, and finally looked up at him.

The rope ended. Henry just stared at her in shock.

"Henkin assigned me to the case," she said, looking evenly into his eyes, not even flinching for a second. It was business now. "He said I could take it or be fired," she paused a bit and then said, "I didn't have any choice."

"You didn't have any choice but to stab me in the back?" His voice went dry and cracked, and it felt to him physically, like somewhere inside his chest, the largest muscle there just broke.

"I'm not stabbing you in the back," Mary said. She reached out to him, stood up, moved in next to him close enough so he could smell her perfume, close enough so that he could smell her skin, feel her breath as she spoke, as close as lovers are when kissing begins. "I'm trying to save your career," she said, "and mine. They outsmarted us. Henry, I don't have a brother who has a big law firm." She said it looking into his eyes with the same look she wore the first time they made love, when she said, I don't have any protection.

"There aren't any choices for a woman attorney. And there aren't any other jobs waiting out there for me, either. You can go into your brother's firm, you can take the damn thing over when he retires."

Then the look changed and if Henry had been thinking of anyone other than himself, he would have thought he had never seen anyone look so lonely, so completely alone. It was the same look he was wearing now as well. "I don't have that option. The only option I had was to stop being a lawyer. What could I have done, Henry? You tell me. Henry this is so unfair."

She didn't hear what he said next. He was already halfway out the door.

Chapter Ten

HENRY COULDN'T REMEMBER having seen Willie look so happy. He looked like a kid waiting for Christmas.

"Listen, Hank," he said, "I appreciate everything you tried to do, ya know, but, I mean, shit, man, it's all too complicated. I don't know half the shit you're talkin' about in there. And what I do understand I don't believe, you know? So why should they?"

He laughed and flipped a card onto his cot. Henry couldn't tell what the object of this game was, but it seemed to amuse Willie.

"And I don't care, ya know," Willie said, "I don't have a chance."

"You sure as hell don't have a chance with Miss McCasslin."

He looked at him hoping it would sink in and he realized that finally it had sunk in on him. Henry knew it down to his bones now, not just with his mind. This wasn't just a game of squash with McNeil nor an employee's evaluation of first trial tried, first defendant defended. This was life and death. This person in front of him who smiled and talked and played and seemed so genuinely happy would be suffocated in clouds of poison rising up from beneath his seat. He would gag on it and die and Henry was his only chance.

"Depends on what kinda chance you're talkin' about," Willie said, and flipped out a Jack of clubs onto a pile of clubs.

"What kinda chance are *you* talkin' about?" said Henry.

Willie stepped in close to Henry and spoke with an air of male confidentiality.

"You ever seen this dame? You just missed her. Ever see the tits on her? She's got the juiciest set of titties I ever seen. I played like I dropped this notebook, ya know," Willie said, bending down and miming retrieving a notebook. "An' I looked up her dress, stared her old pie right in the eye," he said and straightened up.

"She had black panties on, not white, ya know?" he said in awe. "I'm gonna get into that dame's black panties before this is over . . . you just see if I don't."

"Willie, we're talkin' about your life, for Christ's sake, and you're talkin' about maybe gettin' laid?"

Willie looked for the first time to Henry as if he might hit him.

"Yeah, I'm talkin' about maybe gettin' laid! I never been with a woman. I got a right before I die, don't I? Don't I got a right?" Willie rocked back on his heels and Henry could see he was fighting back tears. "It's a damn sight nicer thinkin' about that than thinkin' about doin' times tables. Or thinkin' about what it was like in the hole. An' you ain't gonna take it from me! You got that? 'Cause I ain't got nothin' else to think about except that gas chamber. That's all I got. That's all I got . . ."

There was silence between them.

"I'm sorry, Willie," Henry said, "I blew it for ya. I'm so sorry."

He started to leave when Willie said good naturedly, "Hey, don't be sorry, man. Maybe she'll blow it for me, too. That's kinda funny, huh? Maybe she'll blow it for me, too."

"Yeah, that's kinda funny."

Henry was getting sloppy drunk at the Top of the Mark, with Hoolihan and his brother, Byron.

"That's what did it for him," Henry said, downing his scotch. "A pair of black panties. That's why he agreed to let Mary defend him. You believe that?"

Byron finished the last of his Manhattan, burped elegantly and said, "Under the circumstances, I'd say he made the right choice."

Hoolihan threw back a shooter. "I'll drink to that," he said.

But Hoolihan wasn't just a drunk, he was also a reporter. He hated loose ends. So the next day, he went to visit Willie. Hoolihan sat on the other side of the partition from him.

"So how you been, Mr. Hoolihan?" Willie said. "What do you want to talk about today?"

"Well, you've got yourself a delay until your new

attorney can get into the case? Is that right?" said Hoolihan, taking out a fresh cigar to chew on.

"Yeah, uh-huh. Miss McCasslin," said Willie, and then added appreciatively, "Great set of tits."

"What about Henry Davidson?"

"Hank's a good guy," Willie said, "But he don't have tits, ya know?"

Hoolihan wheezed out a laugh and then said, "So you don't care about the fact that the kid lost it all over this case? Lost his job, lost his girl . . ."

"Wait a second. What are you talkin' about?" asked Willie.

"He lost his job," Hoolihan said. "Didn't you know that?"

Willie looked confused. "No, I didn't know nothin' about . . . They just said they were assigning somebody else, this Miss McCasslin," he said. "So, I figure, okay, I knew he was kinda pissed off, but . . ."

"What about Miss McCasslin?" asked Hoolihan, watching Willie closely.

"What about her?"

"She was his fiancée," said Hoolihan. "You didn't know that, either?"

"No," said Willie. "No, I didn't."

The first thing Mary noticed on her next visit to Willie's cell was that he couldn't seem to hold the notebook she had given him, nor the pencil, nor it seemed much of anything else. Whatever was in his hands would promptly be dropped and then Willie would bend down to pick up the fallen object and spend an inordinately long time retrieving it, all the while looking up towards her instead of at the floor. She crossed her legs, but Willie was being unabashed in his efforts to look up her skirt.

"Mr. Moore!" Mary said, indignantly.

"Call me, Willie," he said with an air of total innocence which made him all the more frightening to her.

"Get up this instant, Mr. Moore, or I'll call a guard," said Mary.

Willie straightened up. "Jesus Christ, Miss McCasslin, all I was doin' was lookin'," he said, with a hurt expression.

"Mr. Moore," said Mary, "I want to set you straight about—"

"Oh, Miss McCasslin," he said, "you set me straight the minute you walked in here."

Mary was *very* flustered. She stood, straightened her skirt and backed away from Willie till her back hit the bars.

"Mr. Moore . . ." she said, holding up a hand.

"Call me Willie, can't ya?" he said and drooled, just a little.

"Mr. Moore! I am not here . . . to . . . satisfy any sexual fantasies you may have."

"You're not?" said Willie indignantly and not a little surprised.

"No!" Mary said, shocked.

"They're gonna kill me anyway, Miss McCasslin," Willie said, stepping closer. "So, I mean, you're not gonna do me any good as an attorney. You might as well be good for somethin'."

"Mr. Moore . . ." Mary said, backing toward the cell door.

"Please, call me Willie, huh? I just want to hear a lady call me Willie."

"Willie, listen . . ." Mary said, reaching behind her, hoping a guard was nearby.

"Willie, yeah, that's it. I just want to touch ya a little," he said, reaching out to her.

"Are you crazy?"

"Well, yeah, sure," said Willie, as if stating the obvious. "It's not gonna hurt ya to let me touch ya a little, is it?"

Mary looked out into the corridor.

"I'm calling a guard right now," she said.

Willie started rubbing his crotch.

"Stop that this instant!" she shouted.

"Stop what?" said Willie. "I ain't touchin' you, I'm touchin' me."

"Guard! Guard!"

A jailer came running up. "What's wrong, ma'am?" he said, reaching for his billy club. "Did he do anything?"

"No . . . no," Mary said. "I . . . I have an appointment, I just remembered. Let me out, please?"

She tried not to look too panicked.

"Here you go," said the jailer, opening the cell door.

"Don't go," Willie said to her. "You . . . you wanna play cards?"

Once the cell door was closed and the bars were safely back between them, Mary said, "This isn't going to work, Willie. You need a man to defend you. We'll get someone assigned. We'll be in touch."

"Was it somethin' I said?" Willie called out after her, smiling.

* * *

The phone rang in Henry's apartment that night. Henry was alone, eating dinner.

"Hello."

"Hi, asshole," came Willie's voice through the phone.

"Willie? Is that you?"

"Yeah," Willie said. "Listen, I don't know what you ever saw in that broad, ya know? I mean, I think she's got some real problems. Got these delusions everybody's tryin' to get into her pants. So, I mean, who needs it? Anyway, at least you know how to play cards."

Henry sat back against the wall. "Does this mean I got the job back?"

"Sure," Willie said on the other end of the line. "Somebody's got to look out for ya."

Later that night Henry lay looking up at his ceiling, much as he had as a child away at boarding school, alone, tracing the plaster cracked along the molding, knowing he was now in the fight of his life, had lost his job, had lost his love, was warned that he would be disbarred and in a desperate battle which all of those whom he respected said that he would lose, and one thing weighed against it. Not a pose this time, nor any childish, sloppy midnight bull session epiphany, but simply this: the knowledge that as unbelievably hokey as it sounded, he was on the right side of the fight.

The next day Henry showed up at Willie's cell not with his usual briefcase but with a rectangular box.

"I'm not much with cards," he said, "but I'm hell on wheels when it comes to checkers."

They played and for the first time Willie actually told Henry something of his life, something other than doing times tables or remembering radio broadcasts of baseball games. It came almost without warning when Willie said, "After I got arrested they put my kid sister into some kind of foster home, orphanage, I don't know. I don't know what happened to her. I never seen her again."

He wasn't playing anymore. He leaned back against his bunk and ran his sleeve across his eyes.

"After my folks died it was just me and my brother," Henry said softly. He had no idea what made him say anything about himself or his family. After all, he was this guy's attorney, he thought to himself, not his friend. But here he was, talking as if just the opposite were the case. "Byron was grown already and, you know, a young bachelor," Henry said. "He didn't know anything about raising kids or anything so they sent me to boarding school. I came home on holidays. Most of the time he wasn't there. I mean he didn't have any responsibility to be there. He wasn't my father, you know. After a while I stopped comin' home."

Willie shook his head and said, "If I'd have had the money I'da taken care of my kid sister. I mean, family's family, ya know?"

Henry looked at Willie. Where did Willie come off feeling sorry for him or judging his brother? "Can we talk about the case now?" he said.

"You never give up do ya?"

"Okay, okay," said Henry, changing subjects.

"What do you think the Redskins are gonna do against the Yankees?"

"Hank," Willie said, "The Redskins are a football team. The Yankees play baseball. Personally I think the Redskins will kick the shit out of them. What do you think?"

Henry sat back and laughed. "Hey, I'm tryin', you know," he said.

Willie just looked at him. He might have a friend after all, he thought.

"Yeah," Willie said. "Yeah, I do know."

The following morning Henry stood before the judge requesting a delay. "Your Honor," he said, "As you know I was taken off this case by the Public Defender's office. In the interim another attorney was appointed and since that time, my client has requested once again that I handle his defense in a private capacity. I am currently in the process of setting up private practice, of getting offices, staff and what have you."

The office to which Henry was referring was a corner of his efficiency apartment and his staff was thus far limited to one employee: himself. But he did have a trust fund to draw on and he figured it would pay for a secretary, investigator, and whatever else he needed to mount an adequate defense. The problem would be freeing up the funds which legally would not be his to draw upon for over another year. Byron was the trustee and it meant some serious ass-kissing to get him to change the provisions. Henry was already working on his pucker.

"I would therefore respectfully request, Your

Honor," Henry said, "that I be granted a six-week delay so that we may adequately prepare . . ."

McNeil was on his feet just as Henry knew he would be. "Your Honor," he said, "this is just a stalling tactic. Counsel is not a fresh lawyer coming into the case, he already knows the case. He doesn't need six weeks just to—"

"You're out of order, Mr. McNeil," said the judge, who then turned once again to Henry. "Mr. Davidson," he said, "you have tried this court's patience on more than one occasion thus far. I don't think it takes one six weeks just to move his papers from one desk to another. I'll give you two weeks."

"Your Honor," said Henry, knowing that serious ass-kissing took more than two weeks, "two weeks isn't sufficient to—"

"Two weeks, Mr. Davidson," said the judge, "take it or leave it."

It was not long thereafter that Thurgood Winthrop walked down the polished floors of the oak-paneled corridor that led from his office to that of his partner, Byron Davidson. Thurgood Winthrop was approaching sixty years of age and was the senior partner, having come into the firm when Byron was still in high school. As successful as Byron was, there was still no doubt as to who was the boss at the firm. When Thurgood retired, it would be Byron. But then they both knew that Thurgood would never retire. Walking alongside Thurgood Winthrop on this particular morning was Ben Harvett, an incredibly short, bearded, former professor turned bureaucrat from Washington.

Thurgood poked his head around the door and said, "Hi, Byron, got a second?"

Byron looked up and said, "I guess so, sure." He had just gotten past the "I guess so" part of his reply when Thurgood entered his office with Ben.

"Byron, you know Ben Harvett from Washington."

Harvett smiled his little ferret smile and Byron extended his hand, offering them both a seat.

"What brings you to San Francisco, Ben?" he said.

Harvett sat down in the plush wing chair and Byron was pleased to see that he had to pull himself forward to the edge of the seat to keep from disappearing. There were few things in life that Byron enjoyed as much as a bureaucrat's discomfort and embarrassment.

"Byron," said Harvett, "this is a private conversation between old friends. It never took place. Is that clear?"

"Is that okay with you, Thurgood?" Byron said, deferring to his senior partner.

"I'm the one who suggested it, By."

"I see," said Byron.

"That brother of yours is making quite a little name for himself," Ben said. "They've heard his name even in Washington."

"I'll take your word for it," said Byron, watching the little man closely.

Harvett went on, watching Byron just as closely. "He is evidently going to try and turn this trial into some kind of circus where he takes on the whole federal prison system."

Byron nodded his head and picked up a pencil to play with. "The boy is free, white, and over twenty-

one. I don't have any control over his actions," he
said, holding his palms up in a gesture that he hoped
would convey the futility of trying to rein in a ram-
bunctious younger brother.

Harvett smiled understandingly and then said,
"But you do have control over his trust fund. Your
brother has taken offices, hired secretaries, all on the
assurance that he is getting money from a trust fund
that you set up for him. A trust fund which you still
control."

Byron glanced from Harvett to Thurgood and
back. "And how do you know all this, Ben?"

"You're not new in the woods," he said, leaning
forward and resting his tiny hands on Byron's desk.
"We know what we have to know. We find out what
we have to find out."

"Who is 'we'?" said Byron.

"Don't give me that crap," said Harvett. There was
no smile now, no more pretense at civility, just a little
man throwing the weight of his superiors around,
ready to punish the rest of the world for making him
look up. "The federal government is *we*, okay? J. Edgar Hoover, the IRS. Good enough for you?"

Amazing, Byron thought, *he's firing the big guns before he even lays out the deal. What the hell's he holding in reserve, Eleanor Roosevelt?*

"This administration does an enormous amount of
work with this firm," Harvett said. "The IRS uses you
for consulting work, you're outside consultants on
any number of projects, and you represent some of
our biggest defense contractors."

Enough of this crap, thought Byron. "I'm aware of
our case load, Ben. What's your point?"

That's when Thurgood broke in, leaning forward to make Harvett feel less conspicuous. "His point is that they can cut off our water, Byron. They don't have to do business with us."

"I can make the point even sharper to you, Byron," Ben said, really starting to enjoy himself now. "We can let it be known to our defense contractors that they're at a disadvantage if they're represented by a firm that's on our shit list. I can have ten IRS auditors in here this afternoon going over your books with a fine-toothed comb. Do I have to go on, or do you get the point now?"

"Byron," said Thurgood, "if your brother wants to be an asshole, that's his business, but if you finance it, then it's our business."

Harvett struck a conciliatory pose. "I'm here as a friend, Byron," he said, "just to let you know which way the winds are blowing in Washington.

"This administration does not need public attention diverted from all the good that it's doing by some kind of witch hunt in the Justice Department. I'm just tellin' you what the score is. You find a way to take care of him," he said, "or we will take care of you."

Henry was wading through the canyons made of boxes that changed the landscape of his apartment from simply a mess to a disaster when there was a knock at the door. "It's open," he called.

Byron opened the door into a stack of files which Henry caught just before they went scattering to the floor.

"Hello, Henry," Byron said, "can we talk?"

Henry eyed him warily. "I don't know. Can we?"

"Oh, Henry, grow up," said Byron as he fought his way through the boxes to the refrigerator and took out a beer.

"Help yourself," said Henry sarcastically.

"Right," said Byron. "I paid for a Harvard education, you just gave me a beer. Let's say we're square." He moved a set of files off the couch and took a seat. "I got a visit today from my partner and from a Washington heavyweight. You've been under surveillance."

Henry retrieved a beer for himself. "For what?"

"For putting Alcatraz on trial," said Byron. "For putting their whole system on trial. What do you think? Their message was a simple one. I control you or they cut us in half."

"I see," Henry said.

Byron put the beer down on the floor and leaned in toward Henry. "I don't think you do," he said. "I'm telling you this so you'll understand once and for all what the real world is like. I told you it was hard ball."

"So you did," said Henry. "And just how do you intend to control me?" He was dead serious now, knowing that Clawson and McNeil might be one thing, but in truth, they were nothing compared to his big brother.

His brother was a shark in business and law was his business and no one was any tougher at it than Byron. But there was more. This case now transcended itself for Henry. It was justice. It was his career. It was both challenge and horror, but now it was family as well. It was him and Byron as it had always been, ever since they were each other's only family. It was Henry struggling to stand on his own and Byron struggling to stay the surrogate parent, the father figure and dominant male. It was not just Willie's freedom Henry was fighting for, but in a much less significant sense, his own as well. It was the last tiny battle with his family to prove that he was a man, and an adult now, to be respected on his own. What would Byron do to control him? What would Byron do to pull him back within the fold?

Byron reached down for the beer and took another swig, then wiped his mouth with the back of his hand. It was as if he enjoyed being in Henry's apartment. Wiping beer off his mouth with the back of his hand was as close as he had come to re-creating his college days in years. "I told them that you were a pain in the ass and that nobody could control you," he said, smiling. Then the smile disappeared and he spoke more frankly to his brother than he ever had in his life. "You don't like me. And I don't know that I like you either. I think you're a self-righteous spoiled brat." He looked at Henry like there was nothing more to add.

Henry was just about to tell him to get the hell out of his apartment and reclaim what was left of the beer, when Byron said, "But you're a good attorney and you're my brother, so if you'd rather work out of an office than this place, and if you'd like Irene for your secretary, you're welcome to move your stuff over to this address. I can't bring you into the firm, but I can sure as hell set up a new one. Davidson and Davidson, Attorneys-at-Law. If you're interested."

"Well, I'll be damned," said Henry and he almost cried from joy.

"Mmm . . . I suspect neither one of us will come out of this thing clean."

Chapter Eleven

THE NEW OFFICES were just past the trolley stop on Fremont, two flights up in a turn-of-the-century office building. The doors were the kind with frosted glass and the names spelled out in an arc. Mary came up the stairs and walked down the corridor to the door that said, DAVIDSON BROTHERS, ATTORNEYS-AT-LAW. She opened the door just as Irene was telling Henry, "The doctor who supposedly would have signed any committal papers died six months ago." Henry's back was to Mary and he was so engrossed in writing notes, he did not hear her come in.

"All right," he told Irene, "I want to subpoena all the medical records for the last ten years then, anybody who was taken off Alcatraz for any medical reason whatsoever. Everything in Kiley's files."

"Right," she said, clearing her throat, but Henry still did not sense another person in the room.

"I, uh, I think you have a visitor," she said.

Henry turned around and saw Mary.

"Hello, Henry," she said.

"I, uh, I'm gonna go down to the corner and see a man about some laundry," said Irene, smiling and ducking out the door, leaving the two of them alone in the room.

There was an awkward silence and then Mary said, "I heard the judge gave you a continuance until you could get set up in your new offices."

"Yeah," said Henry. "My brother finally got what he wanted, sorta. We're in business together at last. How are things over at the PD office?"

He started to offer her some coffee, anything to give him a prop, anything to keep the talk small and lightweight.

But Mary said, "I've been doing some thinking."

"Me, too."

"Me first."

"Okay," said Henry, relieved.

Mary got that old, straight-ahead look in her eye, the one she wore when she was not about to beat around the bush but go straight through it. "I worked awfully hard to become a lawyer, Henry, and I'm not going to give that up," she said.

You made that pretty apparent already, Henry thought, *you coming here to rub it in?*

He was ready to have the knock 'em down, drag 'em out, kiss-off scene of all kiss-off scenes, when she said, "And I love you, too and I'm not going to give you up. That's me . . . my decision . . . now I guess you've got to make yours. I, uhh . . . brought you something." She pulled a file out of her briefcase and handed it to Henry. He read through it quickly.

"Derek Simpson," he read aloud. "What—"

"He might turn out to be useful," Mary said. "I'd appreciate it if no one found out how you got it. It could cost me my job, but I figured I owed it to you." She turned and started to leave. Henry reached out and took her by the arm.

"Mary, could we go somewhere and . . . ?"

"I have to get back to the office. I've got depositions and . . ."

"How about tonight? I want to talk and . . ."

She was wearing that perfume and she looked gorgeous. "My cousin's staying with me," she said. "She's up from Bakersfield."

"Oh . . . right," said Henry. She didn't want anything to do with him. He had blown it. He had pushed too hard too soon and scared her off, he thought.

"I could come by your place for a while," she said. She wanted him. He had played it perfectly. She was putty. "How about nine-thirty," he said. "Right after I go to see this guy if he's around."

"He's around," said Mary. "I checked. And he could make the kind of surprise witness who might really help."

"Thanks," Henry said and he moved to kiss her when there was a knock at the door. It was Irene. She had another box of files which had just been delivered downstairs. "Sorry," she said. "They just came by with these files and I didn't want . . ."

"That's okay," said Mary, "I've got to be going anyway. I'll see you tonight, Henry."

"Thanks again," he said, and when she was gone, the smell of her perfume still filled the air. Finally, he

turned to Irene and said, "Irene, go through civil service and see what you can get me on this guy Derek
Simpson and, uh, do it discreetly. I don't want the
DA's office to get wind of it at all. He could be a
good surprise witness."

"You got it," said Irene, with the look of a mother
whose grown son has finally found himself a nice
young lady.

The address Mary gave for Simpson was at 37 Cole
Street. Henry pulled up in his car and got out, not
paying any attention to the car that was parked far-
ther down the alley. The fog blanked out any hint of
a moon and the darkness was palpable, thick enough
to feel, just like the fog. Henry went up the stairs to
the landing of the apartment. He knocked on the
door. There was no answer. He knocked again and
the door gave way, creaking open just a crack.

"Mr. Simpson," Henry called. "Mr. Simpson, are
you in there?"

There was no answer. Henry pushed the door just
a bit and went in. The lights were off in this grimy
little apartment. There was a long entrance hallway
that led to a living room. Henry walked gingerly
through it, calling out, "Mr. Simpson . . ." As he
entered the living area, Henry saw the outlines of a
room that had been turned topsy-turvy. Broken fur-
niture was littered about the floor. So was Mr. Simpson. He moaned as he looked at Henry. There was
just enough light shining through the window from
the apartment across the alleyway for Henry to see
that Simpson's face was a mass of blood. Henry took

a step towards him and then the hands grabbed his throat from behind, and he felt the knee come up into his kidney, crashing into it so hard that he saw lightning flashes across his closed eyes.

Then he felt himself being thrown across the room into the wall. A hand grabbed his shoulder and turned him around and a fist slammed into his stomach, doubling him over, bringing his lunch, his breakfast, and what was left of the dinner from the night before, up into his throat, as the knee came up into his face, hitting his nose and eye, so that the lightning flashes were replaced by red, red that he could taste, red that he could feel gurgling back into his throat and flowing down his face and then another fist slammed into his eye and shut it, crumbled it, sent him to the dark side of the moon, where everything was black and nothing had weight and he floated on the dull pain that was all around him.

He came to, staring up into hamburger meat and then realized it was the face of a man seen through his own bloodied, swollen half-shut eyes.

Henry stood behind Simpson who was dousing his face in the sink, washing off the blood. Henry had a towel held to his own lip and nose and eye.

"Did this guy say anything?" Henry asked.

"He didn't need to," said Simpson, "It was Glenn who sent him, but go try and prove it, they'd laugh you out of court."

Henry put his towel under the spigot, soaked it, and then put it back underneath his nose to stanch the bleeding. "Mr. Simpson," he said through the wet towel, "you feel like running . . . or getting even?"

* * *

Later that night, Henry, still nursing his wounds, got
out of his car and limped toward his building. He
noticed a large, evil-looking man following him.
Henry quickened his pace, looking over his shoulder,
until he reached the door to his building and fumbled
for the key as the big man drew closer. Finally, the
door opened and Henry entered.

Henry stood on the second floor landing just putting his key into the door of his apartment when a
hand came down onto his shoulder. He had been
beaten enough tonight. He whirled around and
slammed the body into the wall, cocked back his fist,
ready to get a little payback, when he heard Mary's
frightened voice say, "Henry! What are you doing?"

"Mary," he said, lowering his fist. Then her expression changed.

"Oh, my God," she said, "Look at your face."

He could feel the blood starting to run again.

"Let's get you inside," she said.

Henry sat on the edge of his bed. With every dab of
alcohol onto one of his wounds, Henry cried out,
"Ow . . . oh . . . Jesus . . . take it easy." Henry
looked up at Mary like a little kid and she melted,
melted into his arms, melted into kisses, melted into
each other, falling back softly against the bed.

Within several hours, however, Henry found himself not sleeping blissfully in dewy, post-coital nirvana
next to Mary, but walking quickly down the deserted
sidewalk to the jail building. He was accompanied by
a very businesslike-looking woman who carried a

court reporter's stenotype machine. The woman's name was Blanche.

Some fifteen minutes later, inside the reception area, Henry and Blanche were arguing with the head jailer, an Irishman named O'Donnell. "Mr. Davidson," he said, "it's three o'clock in the morning, for Christ's sake."

"I know that," said Henry, "but this man is on trial for his life. Now, I have brought a court reporter down here to take a statement from him regarding a new piece of evidence which just came into my hands. I mean, we're not talking about a traffic ticket here."

"All right," O'Donnell said wearily, "all right."

He showed them to the consultation room where Blanche set up her stenotype. After half an hour, O'Donnell brought Willie down into the room. Henry thanked him and said that everything that was about to be discussed fell under the protection of confidentiality afforded by the attorney-client relationship. O'Donnell couldn't have cared less, he wanted to go to sleep anyway. "He's all yours," O'Donnell said, and left, locking the door behind him per regulations.

Once he was gone, Willie turned to Henry and asked, "What is all this, Henry? What's goin' on? What's this new evidence?"

"This doesn't have anything to do with new evidence," Henry said.

Just then, Willie finally noticed Henry's bruised and swollen face. "Jesus," he said, "what happened to you?"

"I was making love just a little while ago, Willie,"
said Henry.

"What'd you fuck, an orangutan?"

Henry ignored the comment. "And I remembered
what you said about never being with a woman," he
went on.

As if on cue, Blanche got up and took off her
glasses and let down her hair. She was pretty and she
was unbuttoning her blouse.

"Willie," said Henry, smiling, "this is Blanche.
Blanche, this is Willie."

Willie looked from Blanche to Henry and back
again. "Hank, you son of a gun," he said. "This is
better than talkin' about the Redskins versus the
Yankees."

Henry put a hand on Willie's shoulder and said
softly, "I can't leave the room, Willie. I'm sorry, the
guard would get suspicious, but I can just turn
around and . . ."

"And we can get acquainted," Blanche said to Willie.

Henry took a chair and turned it to face the door.
He stuck his feet up against the door, as much to bar
the way as to rest them. Then he pulled a book out of
his briefcase. It was a Dashiell Hammett detective
story and he started to read.

Blanche slipped her panties off from under her
dress and then laid down on the floor. Willie stood
there looking at her.

"Come on, honey," she said, "we don't have all
night."

Very slowly and tentatively, he lay down next to
her. Henry could hear the zipper open and then the

sound of Willie on top of her, thrusting, and the sound of his knees knocking against the wooden floor, and then Blanche saying, "Ow. Jesus, my back."

"I'm sorry," said Willie.

"Honey," Blanche said, "you got to get it up first. That's like tryin' to stick an oyster into a slot machine, ya know. Gimme that," she said, and rolled him over onto his side. Willie stared down at her hand as she pumped away at him, working with grim determination.

"Come on, honey," she said, through gritted teeth.

By this time, Henry was getting nervous as well. He checked his watch and then whispered to himself, "Come on, Willie."

Willie had his eyes shut tight. For her part, Blanche knew a lost cause when she saw one but she was not one to throw in the towel. Her head went down onto Willie's crotch, then she looked up at Henry and said, "This is gonna cost extra, ya know."

By this time Henry had his eyes shut tight as well. "Just do what you have to do," he said.

Blanche's head was starting back down again, when Willie broke down crying. He lifted her head up off of him and turned his face away from her.

"I'm sorry," he said, trying to hide behind his arm from her, "I'm sorry . . ."

And suddenly, Blanche, the hardest of whores, softened and said softly in barely a whisper so that only Willie could hear her, "Hey, come on. You got a guard standing outside, another guy in the room . . ."

"Could you just hold me? Please . . . ?"

Blanche pulled him to her breast and rocked him softly. "Shhh . . ." she whispered, "Shhh, baby, it's okay . . ."

Chapter Twelve

"YOUR HONOR," Henry said, "the defense calls Associate Warden Milton Glenn."

There was a buzz in the courtroom. Henry looked at the pieces of paper Mary gave him, and then at Mary, who sat in the first row and smiled back at him.

"Call Milton Glenn," said the bailiff.

Glenn stepped up through the railing and walked past Henry. He wore a blue suit and looked like nothing so much as a muscular undertaker. As he reached Henry, however, his face had the look of a Spanish Inquisitor, a mixture of self-righteousness and sadism. "Run into a door, counselor?" he said to Henry under his breath.

"Fuck you in your lungs," said Henry, just loud enough for Glenn alone to hear.

The way Glenn looked at him, Henry knew that if he had been a prisoner at Alcatraz, he would be dead, and more than that, that death would have been the least of his problems.

After Glenn took the oath and stated his name,

Henry asked, "You are the Associate Warden of Alcatraz, is that correct?"

"That's right," Glenn said.

"And as such," said Henry, "you are responsible for the day-to-day running of the prison?"

Glenn puffed up his chest and said, "You could say that."

Henry pulled out a piece of paper. "Mr. Glenn," he said, "I show you a list with thirty-two names on it which we would like to be marked Defense Exhibit *A.*"

He handed a copy of the list to the bailiff to be marked and a copy to Glenn.

"These are the names of men who were all prisoners at Alcatraz during your tenure there," Henry said. "Is that correct?"

Glenn let a little smile play across his lips. "I don't remember the name of every prisoner so—"

Henry cut him off. "Well, I have committal papers with your signature on them as well as the signatures of Doctors Kiley and Rasmussen," he said. "Now all of these men were taken off Alcatraz in straightjackets and placed in mental institutions. Is that correct?"

Henry didn't realize it, but he was bouncing on his toes like a boxer.

"Objection, Your Honor," McNeil said. "Question is immaterial."

Henry turned to the judge and decided to go for broke and put it in language the jury could understand.

"Your Honor," he said, "I am saying in lay terms that Alcatraz drives people insane." He turned to the jury and added "Crazy. It makes people crazy." Then he turned back to the judge. "I'm saying that it has already done so in thirty-two instances. Now if that's not true, this witness should have the chance to say so. If it is true, it is most material and the jury ought to be privy to that as well."

Clawson glanced at his own notes and was about to rule against Henry when Glenn sniggered, not just derisively but loudly. Clawson shot him a look that said in this venue, *he* was God, and he didn't care for sniggering. "Objection overruled," he said.

Henry smiled. "Thank you, Your Honor," he said, turning to Glenn. "Is it not true that these men were taken off Alcatraz in straightjackets and placed in mental asylums, and that you and whoever was prison doctor at the time signed the committal papers and transfer papers."

"True," said Glenn, with his jaw jutting out as if to say, Come on punk, hit me, you're so tough? Hit me!

"Is it not also true," Henry said, "that of the thirty-two men taken off Alcatraz in straightjackets, twenty-eight of them had never been in mental institutions?"

"I don't know," said Glenn, folding his arms across his chest.

"I have their records if you'd like to see them," Henry said, politely.

"I'll take your word for it," Glenn said.

Henry stepped back and spoke to the jury as much as to Glenn. "So, here are men who came to Alcatraz legally sane," he said, "who were subjected to the conditions of Alcatraz, and then were deemed to be insane. Is that not also true?"

"Yeah, but you can't say one thing caused the

other!" said Glenn, waving his hand as one would at a gnat.

"Insanity isn't catching, is it?" said Henry. "It's not a virus, is it?"

The jury laughed.

"Objection, Your Honor, the witness is not a psychiatrist," said McNeil.

"Sustained," said the judge.

"Well," said Henry, trying to sound reasonable, "what is there about Alcatraz that could drive a person insane, Mr. Glenn?"

"Objection," said McNeil.

"Sustained," said the judge. "You will confine your questions to areas of Mr. Glenn's expertise, Counselor."

Henry couldn't have cared less about the objections. The jury was starting to go with him now and the judge had inadvertently handed him another cue line.

"Areas of Mr. Glenn's expertise," said Henry. "Very well." He crossed to Glenn. "What are the dungeons, Mr. Glenn?" Henry asked, looking him right in the eye.

"Beats me," said Glenn. "I never heard of them," he said to the jury.

Henry produced a pile of photos from the file at his table. "Your Honor," he said, "The defense offers these photographs as Defense Exhibits *B, C, D, E,* and *G.* Are these photographs of the lower cells?" he asked Glenn, showing him the pictures.

"Oh, the *lower* cells. Is that what you were talkin' about?" Without realizing it, Glenn was starting to sound more and more like a gangster.

"Are there any light fixtures in that cell?" Henry asked sharply.

"I don't recall," Glenn said.

"Look at the photographs, Mr. Glenn, of the ceilings, the walls. See any light fixtures there?" Henry said, bouncing up on his toes again.

"No," said Glenn.

"What color is the cell painted?"

"Black."

"Uh-huh," said Henry, moving rhythmically now like a fighter finding his jab. "Look at the door in that picture. Where is the observation window, as you call it? It's a peephole, isn't it, about the size of a dime?"

"I don't know how big it is," Glenn said, leading with his chin again.

"How much light comes into that pitch-black cell with no window when the door is closed?"

"Not much," Glenn said.

"How long was Willie Moore held in such a cell?" Henry said, stepping back.

"I don't recall exactly . . ."

Then Henry leaned in and said, "Three years and two months, Mr. Glenn. I have the records to prove it if you'd like to see them."

"That sounds right," said Glenn, who was leaning back away from Henry now.

"Three years," said Henry. "And how often was Willie Moore let out of that cell for exercise?"

"I don't recall," said Glenn.

Henry turned his back on Glenn and spoke now right to the jury box. "Willie Moore does," he said.

"He was let out thirty minutes a year. Is that not true?"

"I don't recall," Glenn said. "And you don't have any records of that, do you?" he said like a schoolyard bully.

"Ever beat a prisoner, Mr. Glenn?" Henry asked, lowering his voice.

"Never," Glenn said.

The jury was with him. Now he had to take them down into the dungeons so they could be with Willie, terrified there in the dark, terrified of Glenn.

"Is it not a fact," Henry said, "that you ordered two guards to throw Willie Moore down a flight of steel stairs? Didn't you beat him? You knocked two of his teeth out, and then—"

"Objection!" McNeil shouted.

"Sustained," said Clawson. "The witness has already testified that he did not beat any prisoners."

"Your Honor," Henry said, "I just want to get his answer down for the record"—he paused and then looked at the jury and cracked out the rest like a bullwhip—"so we can show him to be the liar that he is."

"Objection!" McNeil said again.

But before the judge could rule, Glenn stood up and leaned over the witness box as if he was about to hit Henry. "Willie Moore's the one who's on trial here," he shouted, "not me! He's a lying, murdering, two-time loser. I'm a public servant!" he said, pounding himself on the chest.

"Silence, Mr. Glenn!" Clawson said, banging his gavel. "Mr. Davidson, the witness has already testified that he did not beat any prisoners."

But Henry showed absolutely no sign of backing down. "Well, then I'll just give him a chance to withdraw that testimony so that he won't be guilty of perjury."

"I don't withdraw anything," said Glenn, stepping right into Henry's trap, "no matter what that lying murderer says."

"What lying murderer are you talking about, Mr. Glenn?"

"Willie Moore," Glenn said. "Who do you think I'm talkin' about?"

Henry smiled and stepped away from the witness box, crossing back to the defense table. "Oh, I'm not talking about Willie Moore," he said. "Who'd believe him? I'm talking about a former public servant just like you. I'm talking about the guard who helped you beat Willie Moore." He pulled a new set of notes out of his briefcase and said, "I'm talking about Derek Simpson." He had nailed him. Who said revenge wasn't sweet? It was sweet all right. Served hot or cold, straight from the oven or over cracked ice, revenge was sweet, as sweet as sex or honey, sweeter than anything he'd ever tasted up till now. It made up for the pain in his lip and his ribs, in his groin and the back of his neck. It covered the taste of bile in hyacinth, oh, it was sweet, all right, awfully sweet.

"Son of a bitch," Glenn said under his breath but loud enough for the jury to hear. He was excused and Simpson was called.

Simpson walked up through the court, glaring at Glenn. When the formalities were over, Henry said, "Mr. Simpson, how long were you a guard at Alcatraz?"

"Two years," said Simpson.

"Who was your superior?"

Simpson pointed at the Associate Warden as if identifying a felon. "Mr. Glenn," he said.

"Did you ever beat Willie Moore with a blackjack?" Henry asked.

"Objection, Your Honor," McNeil said. "This has no bearing . . ."

Henry looked up at the judge and spoke softly, not like a cocksure fighter but like a choirboy. "Your Honor, beatings have a bearing on a man's state of mind, three years of darkness has a bearing on a man's state of mind. Starvation has a bearing on a man's state of mind. Does a person have to be a psychiatrist to know that? You know that, Your Honor. I know you do." He paused and then said again, "I know you do."

"Objection overruled," said the judge.

"Exception," McNeil said, and this time Clawson turned on him in genuine annoyance. "Your exception has been noted, Mr. McNeil. Witness will answer the question."

Henry nodded his head in silent gratitude to the judge and then turned back to Simpson. "Did you ever beat Willie Moore with a blackjack?"

"Yes," said Simpson, and as he said it he choked back a sob.

But Henry was merciless, treating his own witness almost as an adversary. "Did you ever throw Willie Moore down a steel flight of stairs?"

"Yes."

"You were ordered to do so?"

"Yes."

"Did you ever have to hold a prisoner named Harmon Wayley while another man beat him?" Henry asked rapid-fire.

"Yes," said Simpson.

"Do you recall a prisoner named Jack Allen?" asked Henry.

"Yes," said Simpson.

The word had barely been uttered when Henry said, "While a prisoner in the dungeon, did Allen not beg you to get him medical attention?"

"Yes," Simpson said, nodding his head and wiping back a tear at the memory.

"And did you not bring his request to your superior?" Henry asked.

"Yes."

"And what did your superior do?" said Henry, his voice rising.

Simpson's voice was hoarse as he said, "He came down into the block and told Allen to shut up, and when Allen kept shouting that he needed a doctor, he opened the door"—Simpson paused like a man suffocating, gulping air—"and he had me hold him while he kicked him and beat him."

"And what happened to Allen?"

"He died, sir," Simpson replied.

"Of internal injuries?" Henry asked.

"They said it was a ruptured appendix," said Simpson.

Henry left Simpson now and crossed to the jury box again, and before asking the next question, stopped long enough to look at each of them, to make sure they were seeing not through their own eyes now, but through those of every prisoner at Al-

catraz who feared every step their associate warden
took toward them.

"And can you tell us the name of the man who was
your superior," said Henry, "who ordered you to beat
Willie Moore and push him down a flight of steel
stairs, who beat Harmon Wayley and beat Jack Allen
until he died?"

"Mr. Glenn."

"And did you ever go to Warden Humson about
these matters?" Henry asked, still looking at the jury.

"Yes," said Simpson. "I told him about Allen."

"And what did he say?"

"He thanked me," Simpson said. "He was real po-
lite and he said he'd take the matter under advise-
ment."

"And what did he do?" Henry asked.

"Nothing to my knowledge," Simpson said.

Henry turned back to Simpson now. "Thank you,
Mr. Simpson," he said. "I won't ask you where you
got the bruises on your face. I already know. Your
witness," he said to McNeil.

"Mr. Simpson," McNeil said, crossing to him,
"while a guard at Alcatraz, is it not a fact that you
had . . . a little drinking problem?"

Henry looked up, shocked. Simpson had told him
nothing of this.

"Yes," said Simpson quietly.

"Is it in fact not true," said McNeil, "that you were
suspended *twice* for drinking on the job?"

It was McNeil who jabbed out at the witness like a
boxer now.

"That was the reason they gave," Simpson said,
shrinking back from him, "but—"

McNeil flashed out an evaluation form, smiling his crocodile smile at Henry as he did. "Your Honor," he said, "the prosecution would like to mark for identification the employment record of Mr. Derek Simpson."

He handed the file to Henry to see.

"Can you recall, Mr. Simpson," he said, "being suspended November four, 1936, and on July six, 1937?"

"Yeah," Simpson replied weakly.

"Is it not a fact, Mr. Simpson," snapped McNeil, "that the reason you were *fired* from your job as a guard is because you were a drunk?"

"That's just not true!" Simpson said, looking up to the judge and then to Henry.

But McNeil pushed on. "And that Mr. Glenn wouldn't tolerate that in a federal prison?"

"No!" Simpson whined.

McNeil had him on the ropes now, moving in for the kill. "Is it not true Mr. Simpson," he said, "that having cost you your job, you would say almost anything to get *back* at Mister Glenn?"

"I wouldn't lie," said Simpson.

"We have your *word* on it," McNeil sneered.

"Yes!" Simpson said defiantly.

McNeil turned to the jury and held out his arms in disgust. "The word of a *drunk,*" he said. "Suspended twice, then fired for drinking on the job—who bears a grudge against his former boss because he fired him . . . for *cause!*"

Finally Henry stood up. "Objection, Your Honor!"

"Sustained," said Clawson.

McNeil said, "No further questions," then crossed

over next to Henry and whispered, "Well, surprise, surprise."

And all that revenge he'd had to eat just came back soaked in acid.

Chapter Thirteen

HENRY TOOK THE LONG WAY back to the office, looping around to the Buena Vista Cafe. The Buena Vista had served as a kind of impromptu office for any number of young men on the way up. Seekers of wisdom and truth had dined on their corned beef hash and poached eggs from the days of Jack London, and their bar generated a warmth of camaraderie even on the coldest San Francisco winter's night. It was also the kind of place where you could pick out a quiet table and grab one of the newspapers hanging over wooden poles from the rack in the corner, and quietly nurse a fresh-brewed cup of coffee with a slug of Irish whiskey thrown in, to take the chill off the fog rolling up from the bay. It was also, Henry found, a fine place to sit and ponder who had betrayed you.

Henry walked up the flight of stairs to the office of Davidson Brothers, Attorneys-at-Law. As he stepped in, Irene looked up from her desk where she sat typing.

"Well, how'd it go in court today?" she said, and then her expression changed. "Oh, my God," she said, her hand going up instinctively to her mouth as she saw the marks of the beating on Henry's face.

"What's wrong?" Henry said, watching her.

"Oh, my God, what happened to you?" Irene said, pushing back from the desk and rushing over to him like a distraught mother whose child comes home from school with a bloody nose, black eye, and front teeth missing.

Irene had, as she told Mary, not only seen Henry in diapers but had changed them. She had been the closest thing to a maternal figure he had ever known. She had devoted herself not to the firm, but to his brother Byron and, by extension, to Byron's younger brother Henry. She reached out to touch his swollen eye. Henry winced.

"They were waiting for me over at Simpson's. Glenn had some of his goons there. I think I've got a couple of cracked ribs," he said, though not in the way of children exaggerating injuries for their mothers, a little artistic performance meant to elicit a wiping away of tears, a kiss on the forehead, a cookie. He was all business now. He had a case to try. "Why don't you call the doctor and make an appointment for . . ."

By this time Irene was close to tears. "Oh, my God, Henry," she kept repeating, "Oh, my God."

Henry put a comforting arm around her. "Why are you crying, Irene?" he asked.

"Oh, Henry," said Irene, "I had no idea . . ."

She clutched at his suit jacket with a kind of urgency, begging not to be judged and if judged, forgiven. "I would never have done anything to hurt you like this. If I would have known that's what was going to happen I'd never have . . ." She began sobbing uncontrollably.

Henry put his arms around her and her head went down onto his chest, her shoulders shaking as she cried.

Years later Henry would refer to this moment as his bar mitzvah, if one equated the final loss of innocence with the true beginning of adulthood. But in truth, it was a different kind of passage. All that was left inside him that was warm was replaced with a spike that was icy cold.

"You'd have never done what, Irene?" Henry said quietly but firmly. "If you'd have known what?" he asked.

Byron was with his partner, Thurgood Winthrop, discussing the proposed zoning changes which would be necessary to expand aircraft production in Southern California, and what state and federal regulatory wheels would have to be greased in order to insure the expansion, not to mention the city and county officials who would need to be massaged. There was a new, idealistic mayor with a greedy wife whom Thurgood suggested hiring into their Long Beach branch office. It was an added expenditure but it could also ease their way through city hall and Thurgood was not above reminding Byron of one of Willard Davidson's favorite dictums with regard to politicians. "Buy 'em early, buy 'em cheap," the elder

Davidson used to say, "buy 'em early, buy 'em cheap." His reminiscence was exploded with the sound of the door crashing open behind the oak-paneled wall behind him.

"Henry," Byron said pleasantly.

But before he could complete his greeting, Henry had grabbed Thurgood by the lapels and was dragging him across the room.

"This son of a bitch gave away my notes!" he shouted.

"Get your hands off me, you simpering little shit!" Thurgood thundered.

But Henry was having none of it. He turned to Byron, still holding Thurgood. "Irene said she showed them to him, Byron! He gave 'em to McNeil!"

Byron now grabbed Henry from behind, his grip made strong by countless hours on the squash court. "Take your hands off him, Henry," he said quietly. "Take your hands off him now."

Henry released him.

"He gave McNeil my notes," Henry said again. "He tipped them that I was going over to see Simpson and they told Glenn and Glenn had his gorillas waiting for me." He was about to turn to Byron and say, Listen, pal, I wasn't the only one who was betrayed here. This son of a lying dog corrupted our surrogate mother, turned her against us, had her betray me and in so doing betray you as well! Put another way, Henry was looking at Thurgood knowing that he was about to sic his big brother on him when Thurgood spoke, cutting him off.

Thurgood straightened his suit lapels. "Nobody

gave anything to anyone. That would be stupid," said Thurgood, who above all else, was not about to be accused of being anything but smart. "I *told* Glenn," he said. "He did the rest. So there's no piece of paper. No proof."

Henry looked from Thurgood to Byron, his head spinning. The guy wasn't even denying it. He was proud of it! He had all the angles figured and he was proud of it!

It was as if Thurgood had heard Henry's thoughts. "No one here is going to talk," he said. "Irene's been with us for thirty years. She knew what she was doing. I admit it's regrettable," he said, enjoying the dazed expression which played across Henry's face. "But this was business. Business, Henry, that's all."

Henry turned to Byron. To his brother. To the only family he had. "How could you let them do this? Byron," he said, "how could you let them do this to me? Not just to Willie, but to *me?* To your brother. How could you just sit by and let them do it?"

And as if a mask had come down, his brother looked at him with the eyes of their grandfather who ate robber barons for breakfast.

"I didn't just sit by," he said. "It was my idea."

Henry felt as if the floor were slipping out from underneath him, felt sick to his stomach, felt like he had when the fist slammed into his mid-section, robbing him of air, suffocating him, doubling him over, gasping like some marine creature who's swallowed the hook and is yanked, throat first, onto dry land to die, gulping back his innards.

"You had to be controlled," Byron said, "I told you it was hard ball, Henry."

* * *

There was no place to go. No one he loved who was
left who hadn't betrayed him. Not his mother, not his
father, neither lover nor brother, not even one friend,
so he went to jail. He went to Willie Moore.

"Your own brother did that?" Willie said in disbelief. "Your own *brother?*"

"Yeah," said Henry. His eyes were red and he
looked as if he'd just been run down with a truck.

"Jesus," said Willie, "rich people are really weird."

They were quiet for a while, neither of them saying
anything. Then, Willie pulled out one of his baseball
bubble gums and offered one to Henry.

"You want some bubble gum?"

"No, thanks," Henry said, shaking his head, laughing bitterly. "Bubble gum."

"Bubble gum's good," said Willie.

They were both quiet.

"Hank," said Willie, finally, "are we friends?"

"Yeah, sure," Henry said without looking at him.

"Is it over?" said Willie, quietly. "I mean, is that all
now? There's nothin' more you can do? With the
trial, I mean."

Henry looked across at him. Willie was sitting
there, playing with the mattress ticking on his cot.

"I thought you didn't care," Henry said.

"I *don't* care," said Willie, looking up. "I mean,
well, as long as you got shit to throw at 'em we can
keep on talkin' and stuff, but soon as it's over, it's
over, huh?"

He looked like a little kid who is trying to be kept
from being sent to sleep.

"Willie," said Henry, "this thing isn't just . . . I'm

not just here to keep you entertained till the executioner comes, you know. This thing is more . . ." He stood up and crossed over to the bars, saying, "Aw . . . what's the use!"

"Hank," said Willie.

"What?"

Willie got up from the cot and walked over to Henry. "If . . . if I was on the outside, I mean, if there was like the good fairy or something and she waved her wand and I was on the outside . . . You and me . . . would we be friends then, too?"

"Sure," Henry said without even pausing to think.

"No, we wouldn't," said Willie, fixing him with his one good eye. "You wouldn't have nothin' to do with me, an' what I can't figure is why, you know?" His voice was choking now, and it was as if everything that had happened in his life had led up to this moment and the question Why. "I mean, we both got nobody else," he said. "We're both the same age. If I'da lived in your house, if somebody switched us when we was babies, I'da been just like you."

Henry looked up at him now as if hearing him for the first time.

Willie looked off, weaving a fairy tale of two babies switched at birth, perhaps by an evil witch who had been insulted and placed this curse upon them only to have it reversed in the end, only to have the ending be as all fairy tales are: happy.

"An' if," Willie continued, "they'da stuck you in that hole instead of me, you'd be sittin' here just like me now, sayin' how come we couldn't be friends? You ever steal five bucks?"

"Once," said Henry, "from my brother's wallet."

"What happened?" asked Willie, seeing in this a symmetry of past crimes, a logarithm that would prove his point. "What happened?"

"He told me not to do it anymore," Henry said simply.

"That's the difference, ain't it?" said Willie, looking back at Henry. "They stuck me in Leavenworth. Why'd they do that to me, Hank? I can't figure it. I mean, I know it's over for me an' I don't care what happens at this trial but I'd kinda like to ask them that, you know?"

It was a question he had never asked. "I mean, why'd they stick me in Leavenworth? Why'd they stick me in that hole for three years? I mean, I coulda been just like you! I'd like to ask 'em, you know?" He was in tears.

Henry reached out and pulled Willie towards him and let him cry on his shoulder. "Okay," he said, "that's just what we'll do."

"Your Honor," Henry said to the packed courtroom. He paused as he looked from the judge to the jury and then out into the full crowd that included newspapermen from every major city and state in the country.

He was about to pull off a move whose daring would be compared, he knew, to that of Clarence Darrow. But this one, he told himself, was not for the gallery or the fulfillment of childhood fantasy, this was simply to keep his word to someone who could've been just like him, if a good fairy or wicked witch had switched them at birth.

"Your Honor," he said, "the defense calls the Warden of Alcatraz, Harold Humson."

"Call Harold Humson," said the bailiff.

You could hear pens scratching against pads as reporters furiously took notes, as artists sketched caricatures, craned their necks, leaned over the rails, strained for looks at one another and the Warden of Alcatraz, who had just been called as a witness for the defense.

Humson himself with his wisp of a Woodrow Wilson thin-lipped smile and college-president demeanor of detached enlightenment turned first to Mr. Glenn and then to Henry, as if to say, Who me? He smiled without showing his teeth, a self-conscious smile and then regained the look of noblesse oblige, a professor turned prison warden, armed with statistics and theories of compassion.

"Do you swear to tell the truth, the whole truth and nothing but the truth, in the matter now pending before this court, so help you God?" asked the bailiff.

"So help me God," said Humson in a truly beautiful baritone voice. He said "God" the way Episcopalian ministers pronounced it, as if it were "Gahhd," a word not spoken as much as breathed.

"Be seated," said the bailiff.

Humson adjusted his wire-rimmed glasses and looked up at Henry and Henry thought, *I can't take him. He's too benign looking, I don't have a chance, I don't know how to finesse him.*

And without realizing it, Henry was talking not to himself, but to his father. *You haven't even asked the first question,* said the voice in his head that he re-membered from his childhood. *How do you know?*

Because I know I'll just look like a smart-ass kid if I try.

Then don't be a smart-ass, said the father inside his brain.

"Counselor," said the judge, "either ask some questions or excuse the witness."

Henry turned around, panic-stricken. He had no business being here. He had no business trying to take on the father of American penal reform. Then he saw Willie looking at him, nodding to him, Go get him.

He turned back to the warden of Alcatraz and said, "Warden Humson . . . Somebody wanted me to ask you some questions."

"All right," said Humson, "I'll help in any way I can."

Don't take him on, said his father's voice in his head. *Sneak up on him, blindside him. Don't take him on.*

Henry smiled, appreciatively at the warden. "War-den Humson," he said, "I want you to understand that it is not my intention to attack you, sir, nor try to impugn your reputation. I have the greatest respect for your accomplishments. You've probably had the most distinguished career of any man in your profes-sion."

"Oh, I don't know about that," Humson said with a good-natured wave of his hand. "Thank you, that . . . that's very kind of you to say so. I didn't expect this to be so . . . so laudatory."

Stay right there, said the voice. "Well," said Henry,

"you *should* be lauded for what you've done. You cleaned up Folsom prison which was a disgrace before you took it over, was it not?"

"Well," Humson said, nodding his head up and down, "let's just say I left it better than I found it."

"Yes, you did, sir," said Henry.

He crossed back to his table and pulled out the file he had compiled on Humson. He had stayed up all night reading every word the man had ever written and ever word that had ever been written about him.

"You introduced vocational training there," Henry said. "Is that not true?"

"Yes, it is," said Humson, smiling despite himself, once again at the memory of the accomplishment.

"You made sure that every prisoner had a right to petition the warden. That was another of your innovations. I have it right here in an article you wrote. Is that not true?" asked Henry.

"I must say, you're making this awfully painless, young man," Humson said, chuckling, and there was a light and nervous laughter that echoed around the room.

"In fact," said Henry, "you introduced the whole concept of rehabilitation into the professional jargon." Henry stopped talking and just looked at the warden.

"Is that a question," Humson said, "or . . . ?"

"No sir," said Henry, "that's a statement of fact."

"Well, then, yes, thank you," said the warden, completely puzzled now.

"Now all of those accomplishments and reforms were instituted before you became Warden of Alcatraz. That's true if I'm not mistaken," Henry said.

"Yes, it is," said Humson.

Nice and slow, said Henry's father, *nice and slow, just like a fish. Don't let him feel it.*

"And Alcatraz was in effect the crowning jewel in your career?" Henry asked.

"Well," said Humson, "I don't know that I'd go so far as to say that."

"Your Honor," said McNeil, rising, "I don't know where all this is leading. I must object. What connection does any of this have to—"

Henry cut in with an aw-shucks air about him. "Do you believe that fella objecting to me saying these nice things about you?" he said to Humson. "I thought you two guys were on the same side."

There was laughter in the courtroom and from the jury. Even Humson chortled to himself.

"I'd watch out for him, Warden, I think he has it in for you," Henry said.

"Mr. Davidson," said Clawson, not joining in the levity, "where *is* all this leading?"

Don't take him *on, either,* said Henry's dad. *Aw shucks and just plain folks, got it, kid?*

"Your Honor," said Henry, "the defense has stated that Alcatraz placed Willie Moore in a psychological coma. In my opening statement, I said that Alcatraz is the one who's guilty in this case. Now I believe that Warden Humson is an honest man." Henry paused and looked over at Humson, so the jury could see him looking at Humson.

It was a clean look without a trace of smirk or smart-aleck about it. "And I believe that if he comes to the conclusion that what I said is true," said Henry, "he will tell us so." He let that hang there in

the air. "And if it's not true," Henry said to the jury
as much as to the judge, "he ought to have the right
to prove that it's not. These are serious charges I
have lain before this court and the warden ought to
have the right to answer them."

"Objection overruled," said Clawson.

And Henry knew that he had just cleared the first
hurdle. He had just placed the warden officially on
trial and said, Answer the charges, you have a right
to, now answer the charges. And the judge had said,
Amen, and now the jury waited.

"Thank you, Your Honor," said Henry. "Where
was I?" he said to the court reporter.

"You were just calling Alcatraz the crowning
jewel," said Humson, smiling.

Again there was laughter. They liked Humson.
Humson could feel it and so could Henry.

Don't attack, the voice said. So Henry smiled as
well and allowed a little chuckle of his own.

"That's exactly where I was," he said, in an awed
tone. "You have a really wonderful memory, Warden,
don't you."

"Oh, I don't know," said Humson, properly mod-
est about his abilities.

"Sure you do," said Henry. "You pride yourself on
your memory, I should think, and rightfully so."

"Yes, I do," said Humson, almost as if he was
happy to be appreciated.

"Now," Henry said, "you weren't just assigned to
Alcatraz, were you? You were given Alcatraz. It was
your baby, to design every aspect, to write the man-
ual, the regulations. Why you even had a hand in
putting the menu together, did you not?"

It was now Humson's turn to look impressed with Henry's research.

"Why, yes, I did," he said.

"And this wasn't an easy assignment, was it?" said Henry, commiserating with the difficulty of the task.

"No," said the warden. "I can say in all candor it was not."

Almost like a mother saying to her child about the splinter in his thumb, 'Cause it's a bad boo-boo, isn't it, Henry said, "Because Alcatraz wasn't meant to be like other penitentiaries, was it? It was built to be escape-proof, was it not?"

"Yes," said Humson, and for the first time, Henry could see a wary, tentative look in his eye.

Step by step, said the voice, *build it step by step and don't spring the trap till it's built.*

"It was built to house the likes of Al Capone?" Henry said, "Vicious criminals. The worst of the worst, is that not true?"

"Oversimplified, perhaps," said Humson, sticking just a toe into these new waters. "Oversimplified, perhaps, but basically true."

"In fact," said Henry, tentatively placing the next brick in the edifice, "part of the idea was to instill in the men the fact that from Alcatraz there is no escape, true?"

"True," Humson said cautiously.

"This wasn't like your other assignments," Henry said. "There wasn't the idea that rehabilitation was the prime concern here. Punishment and incarceration were the core of the assignment, in fact, is that pretty much true, Warden?"

Don't give him anything to argue with, kid. He's got to agree with everything you say until you're set.

"I think one can say that," said Humson.

"If a prisoner is doing life on the Rock, he will die on the Rock." He looked up for the tiniest moment at the jury to see if they were with him as well.

"We try to discourage any hope for escape," said Humson, who unconsciously looked now to the jury himself, as if to further explain.

"And that's why Willie Moore was in fact put into the dungeon," Henry said, "so that the rest of the population would take a lesson from his folly."

Humson thought that one over. He was not about to give a yes or no. "Part of the consideration was to prevent further escapes." Henry was about to ask another question when suddenly, as if he had just remembered something he had long ago intended to ask, he said, "Oh, by the way, you don't have any children, do you?"

"Children?" said the warden, obviously thrown by the query. "No. I don't see what that has . . ."

Henry let the aw-shucks tone slip and said, "Just answer the question please, Harold. Do you have children?"

"No," said Humson, "No, I don't. My career always took precedence."

"I just wondered," Henry said, "weren't the guards and the prisoners, in fact, like a kind of family to you?"

"Well, I don't know that . . ." Humson said, very wary of him now.

Tread easy, said the voice, *you're not ready yet. Almost . . . but not quite yet.*

"Well, now in a book you wrote . . ." said Henry, "I don't have it with me, I can get a copy if you like, but you have such a good memory I'm sure you'll remember it . . . you referred to the convicts as children, as *your* children, in fact, and you likened your job to that of a parent, to providing for their physical needs and molding their character."

"I'd say you don't have a bad memory yourself, son," Humson said, trying to out aw shucks him. "That's exactly what I wrote."

"In fact," said Henry, "that's probably why you took such care about the physical needs of the prisoners. Not many people realize this, but Alcatraz is the most expensive federal prison we have, isn't it?"

Humson looked around, hesitantly, as if afraid that he was going to be asked to justify his budget. "Yes," he said, "I believe so."

"I'm not finding fault," said Henry.

Attaboy, said the voice, *let him take more line. Just a little bit more . . . just the tiniest bit more.*

"I'm not finding fault at all," Henry repeated, "but people don't know. The food for instance, at Alcatraz, is superior, is it not?"

"Yes it is," said Humson, with obvious pride.

Now, said the voice, *give him a tug.*

"Except in the dungeon," Henry said, glancing up at the jury again.

"I never referred to any cell as—"

"Well, you know what I'm talking about, don't you?" said Henry, cutting him off.

"The lower cells," Humson said defiantly.

"So the food at Alcatraz was superior . . . except in the lower cells."

"That's because those were punishment cells," said Humson.

But Henry cut him off again, sharply this time, "So your answer is 'yes'?"

"Yes," said the warden.

"And Alcatraz is immaculately clean." said Henry. "Except for the lower cells."

"Yes," Humson said again.

"All prisoners have the right to petition the warden," Henry said, ticking off another privilege just before making it disappear once again. "Except those in the dungeons. Is that correct?"

"Yes."

"So in fact," said Henry, crossing to the jury, "there were two prisons. There was Alcatraz and there were the dungeons."

"No," Humson said, getting agitated, "that's not true. The lower cells were just a minor tool in the overall picture of Alcatraz. The isolation or solitary confinement cells were simply a tool of a temporary nature for extreme cases within the general population."

Humson turned to the jury. It was they who needed to understand him, and nothing could be more reasonable than the explanation he was offering. They didn't know what it was like. He just had to make them see, that's all. Educate them. "In every inmate population," he said, "you have extreme cases which call for extreme measures."

"And who oversaw the day to day running of the dungeon section," said Henry, and then corrected himself: "I'm sorry. The lower cells."

"The associate warden, Mr. Glenn," said Humson,

"who I believe has been much maligned here by a former—"

Again Henry cut him off. "You're getting ahead of me, Warden, I didn't ask that," Henry said. "So it's an extreme measure for extreme cases, is that correct?"

"Yes," said Humson, as if nothing could be more correct than that.

"I have here a record of a prisoner named Johnson who did a total of fifteen hundred days in the lower cells, the hole, the dungeon, over a ten-year period, for such offenses as not finishing all the food on his plate, having an extra pair of socks in his cell, keeping an untidy cell, smuggling food from the dining room—crumbs in fact—to a pet lizard. Are these the extreme cases that warranted fifteen hundred days in pitch darkness with food served only every third day?"

"They were extreme when one is trying to instill a respect and obedience for every regulation, no matter how big or small," Humson said.

"Total obedience?" asked Henry.

"Yes," said Humson, getting testy. He knew exactly where this smart aleck was trying to take him. "Total obedience. Moreover, may I say something?"

Henry was about to say, No, I'll ask the questions, when his father's voice said, *Let him talk.*

"By all means," said Henry.

"You make it sound," said Humson, "like this prisoner did fifteen hundred days at one stretch for one infraction. Prisoners were held for nineteen days at a time. That's all."

Now, said the voice. "Well," said Henry. "Why

didn't you hold him for a thousand days for not making his bed?"

"Because," Humson said, "that would be absurd."

"Or inhuman?" Henry asked, as his father patted him on the shoulder and said, *Now, get him now!*

"Yes," said Humson. "That would be inhuman."

Now the aw shucks was completely gone, as Henry spoke in a voice of Old Testament prophets, with righteous indignation.

"Willie Moore did more than one thousand days in the dungeons," he said. "One thousand days in total darkness. Not nineteen days, but one thousand days with only thirty minutes of daylight a year!"

"Yes," said Humson, "but he tried to escape. You cannot compare his offense with that of smuggling food to a lizard!"

"Nor possibly," said Henry, "could you compare its effect?" He stopped and held his breath. Here he was, right at the pivot point of his whole case, and Humson knew it, too.

"I don't know what you mean," said Humson.

"Well, it's very simple, Warden," Henry said. "You're a master penologist. You deemed that any infraction of the rules, great or small, was to be dealt with, with severity, to instill in the prisoners the hopelessness of breaking a rule at Alcatraz. You set the punishment at nineteen days in your master plan, before you ever opened for business, did you not?"

Humson could see the copy of the master plan that Henry pulled out of his briefcase as he crossed back to the defense table.

"I still don't see what you're getting at," he said.

"Did you also at that time, set three years in the

dungeons as the penalty for trying to escape?" asked Henry.

"Of course not," said Humson.

"This was the first time a sentence of three years in the hole had been imposed, was it not?"

"It wasn't a sentence," Humson said. "It was an administrative decision."

"To put him in the hole for three years?" Henry said, his voice rising till it cracked, his arms outstretched in total disbelief. And for the first time, Henry saw Willie. Not glanced at him, not looked at him in passing, but saw him sitting there at the defense table with his ruined eye and caved-in face, sitting, no longer bored, no longer playing with trading cards, but looking up at Henry with a kind of adulation that Henry had never seen directed at him from any living soul. He had seen such a look once before and was trying to place it and then he remembered. He hadn't seen the look, he had felt it, for it was a look he once wore himself. It was in a schoolyard and Byron was supposed to pick him up from school.

Byron was in high school and Henry was in first grade or maybe second. And someone had punched Henry, a bigger kid, a fourth grader had punched him and hurt him, humiliated him and ridiculed him, and Henry had said, You just wait till my big brother gets here. And then Byron had come and the fourth grader who had looked so big now looked up at Byron who grabbed him by his shoulder and said, Why don't you pick on somebody your own size?

That was the look that Willie had on his face, looking at Henry now. The look that said, as he glanced

at Humson, You just wait asshole, you just wait. My
big brother's here now. My big brother Henry.

Henry turned back to Humson.

"Tell me something, Warden," he said. "When Willie was in that dungeon, in that hole in the wall waiting to be let out, did you receive any petitions from
him during that entire time?"

"Petitions weren't allowed in solitary," Humson
said, feeling himself being dragged inexorably towards a cliff.

"Did you grant him an interview?" Henry said,
glowering.

"Interviews were not allowed."

"Why not?" Henry all but whispered.

"Because," said Humson, and now his voice took
on a kind of whine, an almost sniveling sound like a
schoolyard tough might make when caught, "because
that is part of the punishment."

"For a man doing nineteen days, not three years!"
Henry thundered.

His hands gripped at the rail that separated him
from the witness box, and the jury could see his
knuckles white, as if it were a fence he was about to
rip to pieces in order to get not at Humson, but the
truth. "It is a fact," he said, hitting the word, "fact,"
with a thwack, like a bat cracking into a fastball,
smacking it over the fence. "It is a fact that you never
considered a punishment of three years prior to putting Moore into the dungeon!" His hand slammed
down on the railing. "It is a fact," he said, and it
cracked like lightning through the courtroom. "It is a
fact that you never considered *not* granting interviews

for three years *prior* to putting Moore into the dungeon!"

He took in a breath and now looked up to the jury. "And it is a fact," he said, turning back to Humson, "that you simply put Willie Moore into that dungeon and washed your hands of him, forgot about him! *Is that not a fact?*"

"That's not true," Humson pleaded.

Henry pummeled him with every question, not allowing him sufficient time to breathe, so that Humson seemed to be hyperventilating on his answers, gasping for breath.

"Did you ever look in on him?"

"Mr. Glenn did that."

"Did you ever review his case?"

"Mr. Glenn didn't consider that the prisoner had a sufficient attitude change."

"But how could Mr. Glenn know if Willie had a sufficient attitude change," Henry exploded, "if he never spoke to him except to beat him, if no one ever spoke to him, if he was treated like your naughty child, sent to his corner of the room, not for an hour or two . . . but for *THREE ENTIRE YEARS?*"

"Objection, Your Honor!" said McNeil.

"Sustained," said Clawson, but both of them knew that it didn't matter, that Humson was in Henry's hands now, as was the jury, as were they all.

Henry walked across the room to the defense table and Humson gulped, wiped sweat from his brow.

So many awful things had come from that table, so many things that should never have seen the light of day. What new cudgel was the boy bringing with which to beat him, what new flail with which to crack

open flesh and lash down to the bone. Henry turned
to him, walking closer and Humson strained to see
what it was. A report of some kind.

"Is this your handwriting?" Henry said like an an-
gel who keeps the doors to Heaven, can open them
or send you writhing down to Hell for the sins that
were written there before him in your very own hand.
"Is this your handwriting?" Henry said again.

"Yes," said Humson and bowed his head.

"This is dated three months before Willie Moore
made his attempt to escape," said Henry, holding up
the document. "You call Moore, and I quote, 'impul-
sive and unstable, yet with a streak of intelligence.' "

Despite himself, Henry felt his voice beginning to
choke as he looked up from the document to Willie,
like a parent who had finally gotten a good report
card. " 'With a streak of intelligence and a strong
sense of personal integrity, which I take to be a good
sign, which may enable him to learn self-control and
obedience and may enable him to take his sentence
one day at a time.' " He paused and then turned back
to Humson and continued reading. " 'If he does *not*
learn to take his sentence one day at a time, he may
become extremely dangerous.' End quote. Did you
write that, Warden?"

"Yes," said Humson.

"Did you believe that?" said Henry like a Baptist
preacher asking a sinner to testify.

"Yes," said Humson, clinging to this as a drowning
man clings to any leaky thing that floats. "And subse-
quent events have proved me right. He didn't learn
to take his sentence one day at a time and within
three months he attempted to escape!"

"Did he attempt to injure anyone in that escape?" asked Henry, his voice rising again.

"No, but—"

"Tell me," said Henry, building once again, "how does a man take an indeterminate sentence in total darkness, with no human contact except beatings, wallowing in his own excrement for three years, one day at a time?"

"It . . . I . . . the thing is . . ." said Humson, looking from Henry to the judge to McNeil to anyone who could help him explain.

"Isn't one of the effects of unrelieved darkness and lack of human contact a total disorientation and obliteration of a sense of time?"

"In some cases, but—"

"How about a case," said Henry, crossing to the jury, talking now to them, making them see the Kafka-like madness of it all, "how about a case where the men who have put you in the dungeon themselves have no idea how long they're going to keep you there? Where there is no differentiation between day and night, where even the beatings are random. Wouldn't that totally and completely obliterate a person . . . any sane person's sense of time?" he asked of the jury. Wouldn't they in fact have gone insane?

He turned back to Humson now. "Isn't that possible?"

"It's possible," Humson said. "Anything is possible. I try not to deal with possibilities. I deal with facts and hardened criminals."

"But that's not true," said Henry, holding up the sheaf of papers written in Humson's hand. "You wrote in your report, right here in your own handwriting, that you saw a very real possibility that if Willie Moore could not learn to take his sentence one day at a time, that he would become extremely dangerous."

Henry took a step back and then pointed a finger at Humson. *"You* were the one who sounded the warning, and then you stuck him in the dungeon for three years and washed your hands of him. And the fact, Mr. Humson, the cold, clear, brutal fact is that the person you stuck in that dungeon had never, never before in his entire life harmed or attempted to harm another human being. That is a fact, is it not?"

"Yes," said Humson pitifully now, "but . . . he tried to escape!"

"And it is equally a fact, Mr. Humson, is it not, that when he came out this man, who had never harmed a living soul, was now a *murderer?"* bellowed Henry.

Humson was completely cowed now. "I . . . I don't know that one can say . . ."

Nail him, Henry heard the voice of his father say, finish him. "He committed murder, did he not? Isn't that why we're here, Mr. Humson?"

"Yes, and that's why . . ."

Henry strode across the room to stand behind Willie Moore, put his hands on his shoulders and said, "And so this man, who had never harmed a living soul, was now a murderer."

"Yes," said Humson. "That's what he's on trial for."

Henry took his hands off Willie's shoulders and walked back to Humson, and when he spoke again, he spoke quietly, soothingly, a priest, a father confessor offering absolution in the dark.

"My last question to you, sir," Henry said, "is whether you in all honesty, beyond the shadow of a doubt, can look at this jury and tell them that there was no cause-and-effect relationship between Willie Moore's three years in your dungeon and his first and only lethal act against a fellow human being?"

Stop talking, said the voice. *Say nothing, not a word, not a syllable. Make no noise at all. Whoever talks now, loses.*

Henry waited for what seemed like an eternity. There was no sound at all in the courtroom, except the ticking of a clock of which they were all aware for the first time. Then, slowly, painfully, Humson began to speak.

"He . . . you have to understand," he said, looking to the jury, "they all have to understand . . . He . . . he tried to escape . . . What else could I do?" He looked back to Willie. "What else could anyone else do?" But he found no comfort in Willie's look so he looked up to the judge. He would understand, he above all others would understand. They were men of a certain age, civilized men and civilizing men, men upon whom the state depended for public order.

He put a hand up onto the judge's bench and said, referring to Willie, "You can't let them get away with that. If we let them get away with that, where would we be? What would we do if we let them get away with that? Should we let murderers run around on the streets . . . ? Should—"

"But Willie Moore was not a murderer," Henry

roared, "Until *you* got ahold of him! *You* created the murderer! *Didn't you? Didn't you?*"

And then Humson saw it, saw it clearly as a man sees anything once the fog which has shrouded it disappears, saw the face of the killer. And when he saw it, all Humson could say was, "Oh, my God . . . oh, my God . . ."

Henry walked back to his seat leaving Humson on the stand. No one said a word and Humson continued to sit there, staring at the vision, staring at it in horror.

"Mr. Davidson," Clawson said quietly, almost embarrassed to be speaking, "do you have any further questions of this witness?"

"No, Your Honor," Henry said.

Clawson cleared his voice. "Mr. McNeil?" he asked.

McNeil looked at Humson and knew it was over. The man was an embarrassment. "No questions, Your Honor," said the prosecutor.

Clawson turned to the Warden of Alcatraz and said quietly, in a kindly voice such as one might use to an invalid. "Mr. Humson," he said, "you may step down."

"He tried to escape," said Humson, trying to put it back together once again.

"You may step down, sir," said the judge.

Humson looked up, confused, and then slowly stood up and left the witness chair, looking for his seat, as if he'd lost his way in a dark, twisting tunnel with no light to guide him.

Chapter Fourteen

EVEN THE JAILER wore a smile. He opened the door to the cell and let Willie, still in shackles and chains, in first and then Henry.

"I hear ya kicked ass, today, Mr. Davidson," said the jailer.

Henry smiled. "Yeah," he said, "it was a good day." He was trying not to look too much like a little kid whose team has just won the big game. He waited till the jailer had closed the cell door and was gone. Then Henry turned to Willie and bear-hugged him, pounded him on the back, ecstatic in his victory. It was the World Series, seventh game, bottom of the ninth, two out and they were ahead ten to zip. It was the Army-Navy game with thirty seconds left and a two-touchdown lead that had even the most partisan fans heading for the parking lot. It was the end of a battle with the enemy in full retreat. They had won and it was over but for the shooting and Henry was ready to shout, We won! For his part, Willie was almost zombie-like, though at first Henry was riding so high he didn't even notice it.

"Hot damn, Willie," he said, "We did it! We nailed him! We nailed the son of a bitch!"

"You did it," Willie said quietly.

"Well, I was pretty good if I do say so myself," said Henry. He had too much energy still pumping through him to sit down, so he paced, his back to Willie, and then turned to him. "But I got the idea from you, partner. You wanted somebody to ask 'em, so I asked 'em. Did you see 'em? Did you see the jury, Willie?"

Willie sank onto his cot. He held his head in his hands and said, "Yeah, I saw 'em."

Henry felt like dancing a jig, skipping, doing cartwheels. "There's no way they're gonna send you to the gas chamber. Most you'll get is second-degree murder, maybe even manslaughter."

But he was not saying it to Willie. For a man who was in a closed place he could still look off into the horizon. "Ten years if we get a recommendation for clemency and you'll walk. You'll still be a young man, Willie. You'll have your whole life in front of you."

"Yeah," said Willie, staring at the floor and seeing nothing but the floor, "Henry . . ." he said.

"Yeah," Henry said, turning to him.

Willie looked up at him and there was a cold fury in the way he spoke, like a man who'd been betrayed by his best friend, sold down the river, like a man who'd discovered a snitch. He looked at Henry like Henry had looked at Byron. "Monday mornin' I want you to get up there and tell that judge there's been a change of plans. I want you to change my plea to guilty."

"Willie, this is a joke . . . right?" said Henry.

"Not to me," said Willie, and his head bobbed back and forth as he held it in his hands, sitting on the cot, rocking to and fro as he had for three years, in the damp and the darkness. "Not to me."

Henry crossed over to him. "But we've got a chance now. What the hell's wrong with you?" he demanded. "We can win this thing."

Willie looked up at him. "It isn't a game!" he shouted. "It isn't a game you can win or lose! Don't you get that? Maybe it is to you, but it's not to me! 'Cause I already lost and you did it to me." He turned his back on Henry.

Henry couldn't believe it. He had busted his ass for this guy, laid it on the line, lost his girl, lost his job and put his career out there as well, and then rolled the dice and with his talent and his brains and his balls, he had won. And now, this cretin wanted to throw it away? "I'm not playing any games here, Willie," he said, "so I don't know what you're talking about!"

Willie was rocking, comforting himself the only way a neglected child ever gets comfort: from himself. "I didn't care what you was doin' 'cause I was dead anyway," he said. "So you want to jerk off, okay, what the hell."

"Willie, you're not makin' any sense."

"Not to you," Willie said, looking up at him, his one good eye blazing. " 'Cause you don't know what it's like." And now he wasn't speaking but spitting the words out, like something vile, caught there in his

throat. "You been talkin' and you been talkin' but
you don't know what you're talkin' about, 'cause you
don't know what it's like."

"What what's like?" Henry demanded.

"ALCATRAZ!" Willie cried out loud, and the word
bounced off cold concrete, echoed through iron bars,
sent shivers down the spines of men who waited,
locked in rooms of steel and cinderblock for judgment to be passed, and prayed on bended knees no
matter what their crimes, dear God, don't let it be
there. Anywhere else but there.

"Where do you think they'd put me to do those ten
years you're talkin' about, huh?" Willie demanded.
"They'd put me back in *Alcatraaazz.*" And when he
said it, the voice rasped like a dull saw scraping iron.
Henry fought to keep from shrinking back from Willie.

"But when it's over," he said, "you'll be alive.
You'll be able to—"

"I'm Willie . . . !" he said and grabbed him by
the shirt, making him see, forcing him to see that he
was real, not an abstract, not something to fight for,
not a cause, nor a case, but Willie, Willie, who had
flesh they could tear, bones they could break, Willie
who was afraid, Willie who hated the dark and the
cold and the seawater seeping through the limestone
rock and the rats and the beatings that came when
the iron door opened and the voice thudded against
the walls, saying, Get him up, and the hands that
grabbed you, slammed you, the blackjack, the bull's
pizzle, the red, blood-red light that burned into your
brain, exploded against the bones in your skull,
cracked you open and killed you time and again and

again and again and never let you die, there in the dark and cold, with the seawater seeping every time the waves crashed against the rock they called Alcatraz . . . I'm Willie!

"I'm the guy who's got to do the time," he said, "not you! And I can't do it. Okay? I can't do it. I can't do it. It's not worth it! Nothin's worth goin' back there," he said, and he cried as he banged his fists against his skull.

Chapter Fifteen

HENRY DROVE THE CAR he had rented down through the Midwest-looking country. It was barren and harsh in the winter time. The road was a ribbon that twisted past poor, ramshackle farms, with winter-dead trees out front and plows buried deep in the snow. He pulled the car up past the mailbox where he read the name and parked next to the clapboard house. He shut off the engine and crunched up the frozen walk, up the wooden steps, iced over and deadly slick, to the door, blew warm breath into his hands, and knocked against the wood. The door opened and standing there was a young woman of indeterminate age and the look of poverty that let him believe she was eighteen going on fifty. She held an infant in her arms. Her name was Rosetta.

"Yes?" she said.

"Mrs. Dial?" said Henry, "Mrs. Rosetta Dial?"

"Yes," said the woman, the baby's tiny fists caked with filth smacking at her face. "Who are you?"

"My name is Henry Davidson," he said. "May I come inside and talk with you a moment, please?"

She hesitated and he said, "It's awfully cold out here, ma'am." He laughed a nervous laugh. "I'm neither a murderer nor from the Federal government, so you have no reason to fear me," he said. "Please, ma'am, it's important."

She looked into his eyes and let him in.

Three days later, Willie was led by the jailer down a corridor to the small interrogation room. The jailer opened the door and Willie saw Henry inside the room as he entered.

"What's going on, Hank?" he said, at first just seeing Henry.

Henry said nothing, just looked off to the side and let his gaze turn Willie's attention to Rosetta Dial, who sat there looking small and foreign, helpless as an orphan.

"Willie . . . ?" she said, hopefully.

Willie just looked at her. "Do I know you?" he asked.

The thin and pale woman, worn from hardship down to her bones, stood up and said, "I'm Rosetta, Willie. I'm your sister."

Willie let out the most pitiful sigh Henry had ever heard from any living thing, animal or human. He tried to open out his arms, forgetting the shackles that hung from his wrists and kept his hands too close together. She ducked beneath the circle they made like a puppy wriggling onto your lap, threw her arms around him, hugged him, and said again, "I'm your sister."

"Maybe there is somethin' that's worth it, Willie, you know?" said Henry. "I'll see you later." He walked out the door without looking back, knowing he had no right to impose himself upon them any longer. He shut the door, leaned back against the wall, and allowed himself to cry.

She had socks she'd knitted for him, sweets she'd made for him, letters from her husband, and pictures of the child. Rosetta sat next to Willie and the two of them held hands. She showed him a picture of a baby held by a young couple. She was the woman in the picture. The man was a pleasant-looking young fellow. "That's my husband Carl," Rosetta said, pointing at the man, "and that's our baby," she said. Pointing to the child, she added softly, "His name is William . . . after his uncle."

Willie just looked at her, fighting back the tears.

"We want you to come home, Willie," she said. "We want you to come home."

Willie looked at her, held her hand, pressed it to his cheek as he shook his head. "You tell Henry that I appreciate him bringin' you and knowin' you turned out okay," he said. "That means a lot."

He swallowed to keep from sobbing, and then he looked up at her and said, so she would know there was no chance for reprieve from the awful sentence he was handing down, "But you tell him come Monday, he pleads me guilty, just like I said." And then he added, "I wish I wasn't so scared of 'em, Rosetta. I wish to God I wasn't."

He turned away so she would not see him weeping.

* * *

When Rosetta told him, Henry nodded and then later found himself standing on the wharf looking across the bay at Alcatraz. He stared at the Rock for a long time and then he screamed.

"How much longer we got till they get started?" Willie asked.

They were in the little conference room down the hall from the courtroom. It was just the two of them and soon the trial would begin again.

"Fifteen, twenty minutes," Henry said. He was exhausted. He knew nothing else that he could say. It was over.

The two of them were silent as mourners at a grave.

Then Willie said, "I don't . . ." and his voice trailed off, back into the silence there between them.

"What?" asked Henry.

"I never did nothin', you know," said Willie.

"I know . . ." Henry said, putting his hand on Willie's shoulder.

"No," said Willie, looking up at him. "I mean, I never did nothin' good. Never accomplished a damned thing I could look at and say, 'There see that? I done it,' and feel good about it."

Henry saw an opening, just a glimmer. "Willie," he said, but Willie didn't hear him.

"Maybe I couldn't have, you know," said Willie. "Maybe it's all hot air. If we'd have got switched when we was babies I'da still turned out to be a bum."

"You're not a bum, Willie," Henry said, forcing

Willie to look at him. "And if you were on the outside, I'd be lucky if you were my friend."

He held Willie close to him, not to comfort him,
but himself.

"I don't know what to do," said Willie.

And for the last time, Henry asked, "What do you
want to do, Willie?"

"I don't know!" Willie cried out, almost in pain. "I
thought I did. But . . . hell with it. Just plead me
guilty. I don't know nothin' anymore."

Henry looked at him a long while, until the bailiff's
footsteps echoed down the hall towards them and the
door opened and the voice said, "It's time."

"This court is now in session," Clawson said, banging
the gavel.

Henry stood up. Willie was not watching him. He
just sat there looking down at his prison shoes. He
knew that Henry was about to plead him guilty and
that the minute he did so he would plummet down as
far as the hangman's rope was long, until it jerked
him back and took him away from Alcatraz . . . and
his sister.

"Your Honor," Henry said, "there has been a
change in plans."

McNeil looked over at him, taken by surprise,
waiting for whatever announcement Henry was about
to make.

Henry looked down at his notes written there on
the legal pad were the words, THE DEFENSE WOULD
LIKE TO ENTER A NEW PLEA OF GUILTY.

"Yes?" said Clawson.

"The defense . . ." said Henry, looking at the

words and then at Willie, "the defense calls Willie Moore."

A murmur of amazement ran through the courtroom, as McNeil turned to his assistant with his crocodile grin and said, "He had the case won and now he's throwin' it away by puttin' that psycho on the stand. There is a God in Heaven after all."

Chapter Sixteen

AT THE DEFENSE TABLE, Willie grabbed Henry by the arm and whispered viciously, "What the hell do you think you're doin'? I told ya—"

Henry pulled his arm away and whispered back, "You told me you didn't know what you wanted to do."

"About pleadin' guilty," Willie said. "I didn't tell you to put me on the goddamn stand!"

Up on the bench, Clawson looked down at them and said, "Is there some problem, Counselor?"

"No, Your Honor," said Henry, vamping for time, "be just a second."

Then he turned to Willie and said, "I want you to tell them—"

But Willie cut him off. "I don't want to tell them nothin'," he said. "I want you to plead me guilty."

"Well, I don't think you *are* guilty!" said Henry.

"It doesn't matter!" Willie said.

"It does to me!"

Clawson cleared his throat noisily and leaned over

the bench towards Henry, saying, "Is your witness going to take the stand today, Counselor?"

"Yes, Your Honor," said Henry.

"No!" Willie said to Henry.

"You want to tell them you're guilty, then you get on the stand and do it," Henry said, " 'Cause I'm not gonna do it for you!"

Willie just looked at him, silently demanding some sort of explanation.

But Henry just said, "Tell *them*, not me!"

"Counselor," said Clawson, "unless . . ."

"He's coming, Your Honor," Henry said.

He turned to Willie. "Tell them!"

"You better ask me the right questions," said Willie, pouting.

"I'll ask what I want to ask."

"And I'll answer what I want to answer."

"Fine," said Henry.

"Fine," said Willie.

Willie got up, shaking his head as he walked to the stand. "Asshole," he said under his breath, "Biggest, stubbornest, goddamn asshole I ever seen."

Willie sat down in the chair in the witness box. It was more comfortable than the one at the defense table, and he had never been this close to a microphone before. He tapped at it with his forefinger and jumped back when he heard the power hum.

"Do you swear to tell the truth, the whole truth and nothing but the truth so help you God, in the matter now pending before this court?" said the bailiff.

Willie looked over at the bailiff. Someone was asking if he would tell the truth, as if when he gave his word, they would believe him. "I do," he said, not taking it lightly.

"State your name for the record," said the bailiff.

"Willie Moore," said Willie, leaning down too close to the microphone so that it squawked. He sat back a bit and said, "William Moore."

The bailiff crossed back away from Willie, so that no one stood between him and Henry. But Willie turned away from his lawyer and looked up at the judge. "Your Honor," he said, "I want to—"

Henry cut him off as quick as he could. "I haven't asked you a question yet, Willie," he said testily. "You want to wait till I ask you a question?"

Willie turned back to him and said, like a carnival mark who's discovered there are no peas beneath any of the shells, "You're tryin' to trick me. You're gonna try and trick me just to win this goddamn case, well . . ."

Henry turned to the judge as well, now. "Your Honor," he said, "will you please instruct the witness to refrain from speaking until I have asked a question and then just to answer the question."

Clawson turned to Henry and shrugged his shoulders. "He's *your* witness, Counselor," he said.

"But he won't listen to me!" said Henry.

"He's tryin' to trick me!" Willie said. "All I want to do is—"

"Silence!" said the judge, banging his gavel. "Mr. Moore. You will wait until Mr. Davidson asks you a question and then you may answer it. However," he said, turning to Henry, "Mr. Davidson cannot coerce you into testifying against yourself. Do you understand?"

Willie nodded.

Then the judge turned to Henry. "And do *you* understand?" he said.

Willie piped up and said, "I just want to—"

And again, Henry jumped in as fast as could before Willie could complete his sentence. "Willie," he said, "did you and I have a conversation last Friday in which you said you wanted to change your plea to guilty?"

"Mr. Davidson," said Clawson, threateningly, "you will wait until I have finished instructing the witness—"

But now it was Willie who cut off the judge. "It's okay, that's the question I wanted him to ask me."

"It is *not* okay," said Clawson, feeling like he had just slipped through the looking glass and wandered into the Mad Hatter's afternoon tea. "It is most definitely not okay. And I don't need you to tell me what is or is not okay. I will tell *you* what is or is not okay. Okay?"

"Yes, Your Honor," said Willie.

"Now," said the judge, "I want to see both counsels in my chambers right now. This court is in recess!" he said and banged his gavel.

"Now you want to tell me what the hell is going on, young man?" a livid Judge Clawson bellowed at Henry, when he and McNeil were alone with the judge in his chambers. The veins were bulging in Clawson's neck and standing out along the sides of his forehead, as he demanded, "I mean just what in the hell do you think you're doing out there?"

"I—" said Henry.

The judge stopped him in mid-sentence. Clawson shook his head and wagged his jowls, never having seen anything like it in all his years on the bench. "Your own defendant is looking to *me* to protect *him* from *you*. So what's going on?" he said.

"It's just that—"

"I mean," said Clawson, unable to keep himself from cutting him off yet again, "just between the two of us, you're an idiot to put him on the stand for any reason. But Jesus H. Christ on a crutch, what in the hell are you trying to do?"

"Your Honor," said Henry.

"You're trying to get your own client to testify against himself?" said Clawson, shaking his finger at Henry. "You're tryin' to violate your own client's Fifth Amendment rights, huh?"

"Well," said Henry, "uh—"

"Well what?!" demanded Clawson.

For his part, McNeil just smiled. It was so nice to be in the chambers of a judge who was attacking his adversary.

"You see, sir," said Henry, "the other day my client said he wanted me to change his plea to guilty."

"Plea bargain to a lesser charge?" Clawson said, adjusting his glasses.

"No, sir," said Henry. "He wanted me to change his plea to guilty of murder in the first degree."

"I love it!" McNeil said, jumping to his feet.

He was already fishing in his pockets for a pen to sign a consent to a change of plea when Clawson said, "Shut up, Counselor!"

"Yes, Your Honor," said McNeil, sitting back down and trying to wipe the smile off his face.

Clawson turned to Henry and said, with no small amount of incredulity, "Your client wants to plead guilty?"

"I don't think he really wants to," Henry said, scratching his head and looking not a little confused himself. "I don't think he really knows what he wants to do."

"Then what the hell are you doin' stickin' him on the stand for?" said the exasperated Judge.

"Your Honor," Henry said, moving over to Clawson and trying the aw-shucks routine with him, "I know it doesn't seem to make that much sense at first blush—"

"Doesn't make that much sense at first blush . . . ?" said Clawson, outraged at the *chutzpah* of it all. "It's nuts!" he barked like a rabid schnauzer. "It's looney, crazy, loco, stupid . . ."

"But, Your Honor," said Henry, "the prosecution isn't objecting so—"

"Oh, no," McNeil said, laughing, "I'm not objecting at all." He all but got down on one knee and said, "Let him do it, Your Honor, please."

"Shut up!" Clawson barked.

"Yes, Your Honor," said McNeil like a chastened pup.

Clawson turned to Henry and stepped towards him menacingly. "Davidson," he said; "you are either showing your inexperience or you are trying to get yourself a mistrial. I don't intend to have this thing turned into a mistrial, do you understand me?"

"Yes, sir," said Henry.

Clawson poked him in the chest with a stubby finger, "Either by design or stupidity—"

"Your Honor," said Henry, "if you please, just let me follow this line of questioning, just for a little while."

"A *very* little while," Clawson said, and poked him again.

"Yes, sir," said Henry, rubbing the sore spot in his chest. "A very little while. Please, Your Honor."

Clawson stepped back and walked across the room and looked at his shelves of law books, as if trying to peer through the covers for some kind of precedent, for anything as stupid as what he had just heard.

"Your Honor," said Henry, pleading with him, "if there was any damage done, it's already been done. I can't screw things up any worse than they already are."

"Sure you can," Clawson insisted. "You're an asshole!"

"Yes, Your Honor," said Henry, accepting the diagnosis. *Shut up,* said the voice inside his head. *Whoever talks first, loses.*

Clawson said nothing.

Henry said nothing.

McNeil said nothing.

Then finally, the judge spoke. "All right," he said, "all right. But you're on a tight leash, Mr. Davidson, very tight. I'll throw your ass in jail for contempt myself! All right, let's go . . ."

Clawson pushed past McNeil and Henry and blustered out of the room in a flurry of black robes swirling, like an angry nun's skirts.

When he was out of the room, McNeil turned to Henry and said in a very good-natured way, "You don't let him rattle you, Henry, 'Cause *I* think you're doin' great."

Back in the courtroom, Willie was playing with the microphone cord, twisting the microphone head back and forth until Clawson climbed back onto his perch and said, "Stop playing with that."

Willie folded his hands back into his lap and smiled like a saint in an alcove.

"Now," said Clawson, pushing the glasses back onto the bridge of his nose, "I am not going to have a mistrial declared here so before we go any further . . ." He turned to Willie and said, "Do you or do you not wish to continue testifying, Mr. Moore?"

"It's okay," Willie said. "He asked the right question. I'll answer that."

Clawson sighed. "You may proceed, Counselor."

Henry stepped towards Willie, the two of them bristling at each other. "Mr. Moore," he said, "Did you and I not have a conversation last Friday in which you informed me that you wished to change your plea from innocent to guilty."

"Yeah," said Willie, nodding his head and on his guard, determined not to be tricked into changing his mind. "Yes . . . I told you I wanted to change my plea and that's what I want to do."

"Why . . ." said Henry, his tone changing now from adversary back to friend. It was a simple question. The simplest one anyone ever asks of anyone else. "Why . . . ? Why do you want to change your plea from innocent to guilty?"

"Because I do," said Willie, like a smack-face brat.

"Willie . . ." said Henry with all the seriousness

he could muster, "I am going to ask you the single most important question I can ask you. It's what this whole trial is about . . . Are you guilty of the murder of Avery Clark?"

"I want to plead guilty, that's what I said I wanted to do."

"I didn't ask you what you said you wanted to do," said Henry, starting to bicker with him once again. "I asked if you are guilty!"

McNeil jumped to his feet, saying, "Objection, Your Honor. He's badgering the witness."

"He's *my* witness, for Chrissakes!" said Henry.

"I'm not your nothin'," Willie said.

"If the accused wishes to enter a plea of guilty," said McNeil, "I don't know why—"

"Silence!" said Clawson, banging the gavel. He felt a migraine coming on.

"Your Honor," said Henry, "the defendant is *not* changing his plea to guilty at this time. He is under direct examination."

"If he's not changing his plea," said McNeil, "then all this talk about some conversation they had is irrelevant!"

Henry took a step forward and said, "I have asked him whether or not he's guilty of the crime of which he's been accused. Nothing is more relevant than that."

Willie looked up at the judge and added his two cents' worth. "He's just tryin' to trick me!" he said, pointing to Henry.

"All of you pipe down!" Clawson shouted. He rubbed the temples on the side of his head. Finally, he looked up and said, "Objection overruled, Mr.

McNeil. Mr. Davidson, that leash is growing tighter
with every second. You may proceed, Mr. Davidson,
at your extreme peril!"

"Thank you, Your Honor," said Henry, and then
he stepped right up next to the witness box. "Willie,"
he said, "let me take this thing one step at a time. Is
it not a fact that I told you that I felt with the way the
case was going the most you'd have to face more than
likely, would be another ten years, maybe even less?"

Willie turned away from him. "You don't give a
shit about what happens to me."

Henry moved around into Willie's sight line. "Isn't
that what I told you?" he demanded.

"Yes!" said Willie.

"And did you not say to me then, that you were
Willie? *You* were the guy who had to do the time, not
me," said Henry. "You were the guy they were going
to stick back in Alcatraz for those ten years! Isn't that
what you told me?"

"That's what I told you and that's what I'm tellin'
you now," Willie said. "Why are you doin' this to
me?"

"Because if you change your plea to guilty," said
Henry, "or if the jury finds you guilty of murder in
the first degree, the state will kill you! That's why!"

"So fucking what?" shouted Willie, almost coming
up out of his chair, and then he pointed to the window and they could see it, there in the distance, in
the middle of the bay. "I'd rather die than go back
there!" he said, pointing at Aleatraz.

Henry was quiet for a long, long time. He crossed
over to the jury and looked at them, each of them,

one by one. Finally, he said, "What did you say Willie?"

Willie turned to him and in turning to him, was facing the jury now, as well. "I said I'd rather die than go back there. Don't you understand that?"

"Yeah," said Henry, "I do." Then he too looked back from Willie to the jury and said, "I just wanted them to understand that, too." He could see it in their eyes. They understood all of it now. That this man choosing between Alcatraz and death, between Alcatraz even for a few more years and the grave for eternity, willingly chose to die rather than live on the island in the middle of the bay. "Your Honor," said Henry, "The defense re—"

But before Henry could finish the word, Willie was up on his feet shouting at the judge, at the jury, at Henry, at anyone who would listen. "No! The defense doesn't do shit, Your Honor, not till I get a chance to change my plea."

Now McNeil jumped in. "Your Honor, if he wants to change his plea—"

Henry was crossing over to McNeil, ready to deck him and ready to deck Willie, too. "He doesn't want to change any—"

"Order!" Clawson yelled, banging the gavel and banging it again. "Order in this court!"

And now Willie whirled on the judge. "And I want you to sentence me to die, goddamn it!" he shouted, grabbing the judge's robe. "I got a right to die, don't I?" he pleaded. "I want to die!"

"Order!" Clawson shouted again, until Henry, striding to Willie, grabbed his friend by the arms and said, "Why? Why, Willie? Why do you want to die?"

"Because I'm scared of 'em!" Willie said, and pointed over at Humson and Glenn. "I'm scared shitless of 'em an' I'm scared of goin' back there! I'm scared . . . I'm scared! I'm scared . . ." He cried like a terrified child and cowered back, pushing against the chair.

McNeil came around from behind the prosecution table and said, "Objection, Your Honor, he finished his direct examination!"

"I haven't finished anything, yet," said Henry. And then, looking up at the judge added, "Your Honor, it's life and death."

The judge looked over at Willie, huddled in the chair and crying. Willie's head was turned so the judge was looking down at Willie's ruined face, his young face cracked open by billy clubs and blackjacks and the judge said, "Overruled." He turned to Henry and added, "Proceed, Counselor."

Henry stroked the back of Willie's head, got him to look up at him, calmed him and said, "Willie, you want the state to kill you so you can stop being afraid, is that right?"

Willie gulped back tears trying to catch his breath.

"Is that right?" Henry asked.

"Yes," said Willie, between sobs.

"Okay, Willie," Henry said. "No more tricks. I'm going to give you a way to stop being afraid of them." He held Willie in his eyes. He had never been this honest with anyone in his life, least of all with himself. There would be no tricks here, no illusions, nor any promises. Nothing mattered to him now but his friend. Nothing mattered to him but Willie.

"Willie," he said, "if you change your plea to guilty

they will get away with it, with all the things they have done—"

"Objection!" shouted McNeil.

"Sustained," said Clawson, whose eyes were focused nonetheless like those of everyone else in the courtroom, on the two young men at the witness box, separated by a wooden fence, who so obviously loved each other.

Henry was ignoring everything but Willie's eyes. "If you change your plea to guilty, you will die. But they won't be able to hurt you anymore," he said.

Willie now looked up at him, paying attention to every word, almost moving his lips along with the words that Henry so slowly and purposefully said. "But if you fight them and choose life, they *will* hurt you again."

"Objection!"

"Sustained."

"And you *still* might die," said Henry.

"Objection, Your Honor!" insisted McNeil again.

"Sustained," said Clawson, and then turning to the jury, said, "The jury will disregard counsel's remarks."

But Henry was talking to no one but Willie and it had nothing to do with the trial or its record, its rulings, or its law. "I'm not talkin' to them," Henry said to Willie, holding his shoulders. "I'm talkin' to you, Willie. You might die but I don't believe they'll be able to keep on getting away with it much longer. The choice is yours though, because you're the guy who's got to do the time, not me. Too many people have made too many choices for you already, and I'm not gonna be another one," Henry said, and then took his hands off Willie's shoulders and stepped back so that Willie was totally and completely on his own now. "Willie," he said, "what do you want to do?"

Without hesitation, Willie nodded and said, "I want to stop bein' afraid."

Henry backed away, turned his back on Willie so there could be no doubt that the answer he was about to elicit for good or for ill, was Willie's and Willie's alone. He faced the jury and said, "William Moore, are you guilty of the murder of Avery Clark?"

Willie looked down, not at the floor nor at his prison shoes, but into himself, into his heart, in order to see past the darkness into which they had put him. Then he looked up at Humson and at Glenn and said in a voice free at last of any fear, "I'm guilty of killin'," he said, "but they're the murderers." He pointed at the warden and the associate warden and finally out the window at Alcatraz itself. "They're the murderers," he said, his voice lifting loud and strong. "And I ain't afraid of 'em no more."

Chapter Seventeen

THE JURY TOOK with them to guide them in their deliberations, a printed copy of the judge's instructions in the matter of the *United States of America* vs. *William Moore.*

"Ladies and gentlemen of the jury, these are your instructions and you must deliver a verdict in accordance with these instructions.

"You may find the defendant guilty of murder in the first degree.

"Without a recommendation for mercy, that verdict will carry with it a sentence of death.

"You may find the defendant guilty of second-degree murder, which carries with it a sentence of twenty-five years to life imprisonment.

"You may find the defendant guilty of manslaughter, which carries a maximum penalty of eight years.

"You may find the defendant guilty of involuntary manslaughter, which carries with it a maximum penalty of three years.

"And you may find the defendant innocent of the charges against him.

"Should you find the defendant innocent of the charges against him, the defendant will be remanded to the custody of the Warden of Alcatraz, there to be incarcerated until he has served out the remainder of the sentence for which he was originally convicted.

"The concept of innocence by reason of insanity is a clear-cut one in the eyes of the law. If you determine that the defendant did not realize the consequences of his act, did not know right from wrong at the time of the aforementioned killing, then you must find him innocent.

"The law does not, however, recognize moral insanity or even medical insanity. It is concerned only with legal insanity and it is within that narrow definition that you must render your findings.

"If you cannot arrive at a verdict, a mistrial will be declared and it will be up to the prosecution to decide whether charges should be filed once again and a new trial sought.

"In order to isolate this jury from the influences of the press and public opinion, you will be sequestered until you have either reached your verdict or until you have informed this court that you are incapable of doing so, or until such time as this court decides that you are incapable of doing so.

"This has been a long, complicated, arduous trial, and this court wishes to thank you for your cooperation."

Chapter Eighteen

As THE JURY RETIRED to their deliberations, the bailiff came over to Willie, who no longer looked afraid. "We have to take you back, Willie," he said.

"Right," said Willie.

Henry reached out and touched his shoulder. "I'll be right up," he said.

"I ain't goin' nowhere," Willie said and smiled and then disappeared with the bailiff through the door.

Just then, Mary came up behind Henry, hugged him from behind and rested her head on his shoulder. He turned to her and saw Byron approaching from the back of the courtroom. Very gently, Henry moved Mary off to the side, as Byron came up and stuck out his hand to his younger brother.

"I got to admit it, kid," he said. "You ran one hell of a case."

He stood there with his hand out and Henry brought his arm around from around Mary's back so that Byron was sure his brother was about to shake and never for a moment saw the right hook coming.

It landed with a satisfying crack into Byron's jaw, sent him flying back over the railing and destroyed two thousand dollars' worth of first-rate dental work.

There is an old saying amongst trial lawyers. It has to do with the fact that a jury is a strange animal and one can never tell what it's going to do. The only thing experience has taught is the saying itself, When they come back quick, they come back to convict. So if you are a defense attorney and the person on trial for his life is one you now realize is the best friend you've ever had, you pray they're out for a very long time.

The jury in the matter of the *United States of America* vs. *William Moore* sent word to the judge, three hours and forty-two minutes after their deliberations began that they had a verdict.

"Ladies and gentlemen of the jury," said the judge, "have you reached a verdict?"

The person they had elected foreman was a stoop-shouldered man of wispy hair and thick glasses, the kind who looks like a put-upon clerk, definitely not the kind to strike moral blows for justice which demand great courage and fortitude. He looked like the type of man who would walk between whatever lines the state laid out before him.

"We have, Your Honor," he said.

"How do you find?"

The courtroom was silent, not even a cough nor a whisper, no one stirring, not a sound but the clock. And then, the stoop-shouldered, wispy haired man with thick glasses spoke.

"We find the defendant, William Moore, guilty," he said, gulping, his voice catching, and Henry felt his heart stop and stomach drop, his head went down and then his eyes shot over at Willie, who was looking at him as if to say, What does it mean? And then, before Henry could speak or even lift his head, the foreman took a breath and went on: ". . . of involuntary manslaughter."

Bedlam, flash of bulbs and crash of chairs hitting the floor as Henry jumped up, shooting his arm up high in a gesture of triumph, as Hoolihan slammed into the *Herald*'s reporter like a defensive linebacker going for a quarterback, hurling himself out of the courtroom toward the bank of phones and McNeil just sat there, staring straight ahead while Mary blew kisses and the judge banged his little wooden hammer.

"Order!" said Clawson, "Order. This court is still in session!"

"Your Honor," said the foreman of the jury above the din, "we would like permission to address the court if possible. This jury has something else to say."

And that, more than the judge shouting, or the gavel hammering, caught the crowd, turned them around, hushed them into whispers and sat them once again down into their seats.

Clawson looked over at the foreman, listened to the silence in the room that came not from threat, but the quiet moral authority of the stoop-shouldered man with wispy hair and thick-lensed glasses. "Very well," he said.

"Your Honor," said the foreman, "we have this day signed a petition, which I would like to read to the court." He handed a copy of the petition to the bailiff who took it over to the judge and then slowly and carefully, the foreman began to read aloud. "We, the Jury in the case of the *People* versus *Moore* do hereby respectfully recommend and request an immediate investigation by the proper federal authorities of the conditions at the federal prison known as Alcatraz."

"Oh, give me a break," came Mr. Glenn's voice from the back of the room.

But the foreman's voice rose above it. "It is our belief," he said, staring at Mr. Glenn and then back down at his page, "it is our belief that those conditions are not only inhumane but constitute a blight on the honor of the United States of America. Moreover, we would like the following to be read into the record of this proceeding. Though we know that it will have no legal or binding effect, we would hope that it will have a moral effect. We, the members of the Jury in the trial of the *People* versus *Moore*, find the institution known as Alcatraz, its warden and associate warden, guilty of crimes against humanity."

Willie wept and Henry held him close.

A prison boat was tying up at the dock. Willie stood in chains, shackled hand and foot next to Henry. Gates, the marshal, was with them, ready to escort Willie down to the boat which would chug across the bay to Alcatraz.

"Let's go, Willie," the marshal said, and he and another uniformed officer of the court took Willie under either arm and began walking him down to the end of the dock where they pushed through a locked gate marked, PRISON OFFICIALS ONLY. It happened so quickly, Henry had not had a chance to shake his hand, let alone embrace him.

"Willie," he called, "I'll be up to see you. Every chance I get."

Willie turned around and shouted up to Henry, "Maybe you could bring that Blanche along for a second shot at it." Then he shivered from the cold and from fear.

"I'm gonna appeal to have you moved to another prison," Henry called out, leaning over the railing. "And I'm gonna file motions to have your original case reopened. I'm gonna petition the President to grant you a full pardon. It's not over!" he shouted.

Then Willie stopped, looked back and smiled. "Willie and Hank back together again, huh?"

"Yeah . . ." Henry called down to him. "Willie and Hank."

Then the marshal who had let Willie stand there, said softly, "Let's go, Willie."

But Willie turned and yelled back to Henry, "I won. Didn't I? I mean for real. I did somethin'. I won."

"You sure did," Henry tried to shout, but his voice broke.

The marshals now helped Willie onto the deck of the prison tug. They were walking him toward the closed cabin and Henry could see Willie shaking in the cold.

"One ninety-three times two hundred fifty six!" Henry shouted out.

Without looking back, Willie called, "Forty-nine thousand four hundred and eight."

*   *   *

Willie sat in the prison tug in the darkness, the only light coming through the tiny porthole filled with Alcatraz growing larger in the distance. His head bobbed back and forth in the rhythm of the boat, slipping over the chop, in the rhythm of a lonely boy rocking to give himself some comfort.

Being led up from the dock towards the prison, there was a little girl with a ball. Her cheeks were rosy and she wore a coat to ward off the chill. She was the daughter of one of the guards, on her way to the Alcatraz nursery school. She looked up at Willie and smiled and waved, as if seeing an old friend.

Then the path led up to the huge iron gates and the small door at the side. The bolts slipped back. The door creaked open and Willie was back inside the walls.

In the yard as Willie was handed over from the marshals to the prison guards, they took him through a sea of prisoners who parted for him as if he were Moses. And then it started . . . echoing through the prison yard and continuing into the block, resounding from all the tiers, the clap, clap, the steady clap-clap-clap cadence of all the men in cages clapping now for Willie Moore who had stood up for all of them and won.

Inside his office, Humson heard the echoes of applause and crossed to his window and closed it. It did not block the sound, only muffled it and somehow made it stronger, so he turned to his handsome Philco radio and turned the dial to his favorite classical station. They were playing a light air by Liszt. He turned it up.

They walked Willie down a corridor that turned away from the tiers that led into C Block. "Where are you guys takin' me?" Willie said to the guards. "This ain't the way to the tiers. Where you guys takin' me?"

He struggled against them, but they dragged him along, down the stairs, down the stone damp steps, into the dungeons until he was face to face with Mr. Glenn.

"Welcome home, Willie," he said with an awful smile. "You know those three years they gave you for manslaughter? Well, I say you're gonna do all three of them in the hole."

When Henry walked into his apartment, Mary was there waiting. "Hoolihan just called," she said, and he could see she had been crying. "One of the guards tipped him. They've stuck Willie in the dungeons."

Henry hired a fishing boat that took him straight to Alcatraz. Glenn was at his desk as Henry burst in.

Glenn looked up and there was the smile. "Don't you Harvard boys knock?" he said.

"If I don't talk to my client within twenty minutes, I'm gonna hit you with so many suits you'll think you were a fuckin' dry cleaner."

Henry was escorted down the corridor to the steps leading down into the punishment cells, the caves they'd carved in the limestone rock that seeped water with every wave that crashed the prison.

"This isn't the way to reception," Henry said. "I want my client brought up to reception."

The guard did not look at him, just continued walking as he said, "Mr. Glenn said you can talk to him through the door. He's not leavin' solitary. He said if you don't like it you can go back to the mainland."

Henry's feet slipped twice on the wet stones of the steps that led down into the caverns that were so dark he had to stand in one place until his eyes could adjust to this underground world: Then they went down the length of the twisting, brick-and-stone-lined corridors until they came to rows of steel doors with tiny peep holes at the top and hinged slats down at the floor. They stopped in front of the cell door that Henry knew was the one Willie had been in for three years.

"Willie," he said, "Willie, it's Hank. Can you hear me, buddy?"

On the other side of the iron door, in the darkness and stone cold wet of limestone walls and floor, Willie smiled.

"Hank?" he said, and pulled himself up to the peep hole, the tiny circle of light that opened up there in the darkness.

"I'm gonna get you outa here, Willie," Henry said, and then banging his fist against the brickwork, "They can't get away with this shit."

"Sure they can," said Willie. "It's their prison, right?"

Henry leaned his forehead against the iron door. "I promise you I will get you out," he said.

On the other side, Willie's head, too, leaned up

against the plate of steel that stood between them and said, "Hey, fuck 'em . . . I won, remember? Not their decision. It's my decision. So I won. You know why . . . 'cause I'm down here with the truth . . . and they can't keep me and truth locked up forever, can they?"

"No, they can't," said Henry.

"Hell, no. I'm glad," he said. "They coulda won, but they didn't. That's why they stuck me down here, 'cause I won, and they don't want nobody to see it. My decision . . . when and how . . . I won."

Henry strained to see him in the darkness. "We're gonna win again, Willie."

"Sure we will," said Willie, who had turned away from the door now and leaned up against the dampness of the wall. "We're gonna carve 'em a new asshole."

"Yeah . . ." said Henry, softly.

Then Willie ran his hand along the cave's jagged edges and part of the limestone cracked and fell beneath his fingers. "It's all crumblin' in here, ya know," he said. "Whole stinkin' place is gonna tumble down, an' we started it, didn't we?"

"You better believe it," said Henry.

"I believe it," Willie said.

Epilogue

WILLIE MOORE COMMITTED SUICIDE. His body was found beneath the single word he had scrawled on the wall with a piece of the rock that had crumbled away:

VICTORY.

Under Attorney General Robert F. Kennedy, facts brought out in the case of the *People* vs. *Moore* were cited by the Justice Department as part of the reasons for their recommendations regarding the future of Alcatraz.

In 1963, Alcatraz, as a penal institution, was closed forever.

A hilarious mixture of
ESP, Manipulation and
Eccentricity

SOLITAIRE
FOR TWO

- Produced by the same team who were
  responsible for award-winning comedies,
  such as Leon the Pig Farmer.

- An extraordinary love story between two
  extraordinary people.

- Daniel is an expert in Body Language.

- Katie is an expert too . . . in Mind Reading.

Written by Neil Mullarky
Price: £5.99 pb
ISBN 0 7522 0886 1

Available from Boxtree Limited

HOW TO ORDER YOUR BOXTREE BOOKS

0-7522-0919-1	Nightmare Before Christmas – The Film, the Art, the Vision	£14.99 pb
0-7522-0886-1	Solitaire for Two	£5.99 pb
0-7522-0617-6	Pret a Porter	£16.99 pb
0-7522-0661-3	Judge Dredd Novelisation	£4.99 pb
0-7522-0666-4	Judge Dredd: The Art of	£12.99 pb
0-7522-0641-9	Judge Dredd: The Making of	£8.99 pb
0-7522-0659-1	Streetfighter II Movie Tie In	£4.99 pb

Boxtree Cash Sales, P.O. Box 11, Falmouth, Cornwall TR10 9EN

Please send a cheque or postal order for the value of the book and add the following for postage and packing:

U.K. including B.F.P.O. – £1.00 for one book plus 50p for the second book, and 30p for each additional book ordered up to a £3.00 maximum.

Overseas including Eire – £2.00 for the first book plus £1.00 for the second book, and 50p for each additional book ordered.

OR please debit this amount from my Access/Visa Card (delete as appropriate).

Card Number ☐☐☐☐☐☐☐☐☐☐☐☐☐☐☐☐

Amount £ ....

Expiry Date ....

Signed ....

Name ....

Address ....

0154.2 · 831463

MURDER
IN THE FIRST

WARNER BROS. PRESENTS

A LE STUDIO CANAL + PRODUCTION IN ASSOCIATION WITH THE WOLPER ORGANIZATION

A FILM BY MARC ROCCO   CHRISTIAN SLATER   KEVIN BACON

GARY OLDMAN   "MURDER IN THE FIRST"   EMBETH DAVIDTZ   BRAD DOURIF   WILLIAM H. MACY   R. LEE ERMEY

MUSIC BY CHRISTOPHER YOUNG   EXECUTIVE PRODUCERS DAVID L. WOLPER AND MARC ROCCO   WRITTEN BY DAN GORDON

PRODUCED BY MARC FRYDMAN AND MARK WOLPER   DIRECTED BY MARC ROCCO